I0681959

Produced by LouLou Productions LLC
Copyright © 2012 by David Carner
Cover design by R. Carner

Paperback ISBN: 0985951486

To find out more about John Fowler, please feel free to follow my author page on Facebook. The David Carner fan page currently holds all announcements pertaining to this series. Also check out www.davidcarner.com for information on this series and any other works. You may also follow me on twitter @davidcarner.

Other Works

Bad Day in Queen's Landing

The John Fowler Novels

The Road to Justice

Sins of the Son

This Thing of Ours

Journey's End

Day's Past

Cold Revenge (Coming Christmas 2015)

Check out http://david-carner.blogspot.com/ for my current free short story, Bad Day in Queen's Landing and any other Queen's Landing stories.

Author's Note: This book is a little different than normal John Fowler novels. In this book, John is writing a novel about what happened eight years ago. The flashbacks in this book cover events that actually happened and not what John wrote about. Please keep all of this in mind as you enjoy this novel.

John and Sam's Apartment
8 Years Ago

Chapter 1

"What do you mean, I have to go to this party? I'm an FBI agent! I have rights! I have a gun and a badge!"

Sam stared at John as he continued to throw his tantrum. She was holding his tux in one hand and had her other hand on her hip. Sam blamed herself for this blow-up. John wasn't one who enjoyed black tie affairs. Truth be told, he hated them. Sam allowed herself a small smile as John continued his diatribe; he was now rambling on about something about the event being akin to torture. Sam had grown up in a setting that was vastly different than John. She had attended more of these events than she cared to remember.

One of the things she loved about John was his straightforwardness. Well, most of the time. Right now, she could do without it. Her eyes danced as he came to, what he believed, was a very emphatic point. It was all she could do not to laugh at his gestures and seriousness on his face over something as trifling as a party. The sad thing was they both knew John was going to the party; he just had to have his small fit, and he'd get over it.

John grew up in rural Kentucky. Sam grew up in a very large house--John called it a mansion--in Virginia. There were similarities about their upbringings, but there were vast differences. John's father was a farmer, and his mom was a school teacher. Sam's father, as John would say, was just filthy stinking rich. Arthur, Sam's father, took his father's businesses and expanded them. He took multimillion dollar companies and made them into multibillion dollar companies. Sam knew all her dad was doing was playing, "keeping up with the Joneses."

Arthur's chief competitor was Archibald Staples, the only man she ever knew to name his company after his own first name. For all the money Sam's parents had, they looked dirt-poor compared to Archibald and Archibald Industries. Arthur had always complained that Archibald was doing something underhanded and dirty to make all the deals he had; but there was never any proof to support those claims.

Sam came back to reality and realized she was getting a headache. John was still going strong on his arguments, and Sam realized he probably had another 15 minutes of material or so to go through before he was done. Sam decided it was time to put a stop to this.

Chapter 2

"You know Senator Cosby is going to be there?" Sam asked.

John had stopped midsentence with that question. He had been in the motion of pointing in her direction. As for what he had said, Sam really wasn't sure; she had tuned it all out. He pulled back his hand he had been pointing with and straightened up. He had almost been in a stance similar to one holding a gun.

Senator Cosby had been a friend to Sam ever since she could remember. He was also the first person in Sam's parents' circle that had openly accepted John. John had always joked that he and Sam were the kids that the senator had always wanted. Sam always wanted to point out that would make them brother and sister...and married, but she always thought better of it. What John was really doing was taking another shot at Bruce, the senator's son.

Bruce wasn't the incompetent fool he sometimes looked to be, but you wouldn't know it some days. John had constantly one-upped him at the Bureau for the past couple of years. Sam had no idea how Bruce was a FBI agent . . .well, that wasn't true. Bruce was an agent because someone very high up thought the senator would appreciate Bruce's career at the agency. Nothing was further from the truth with the senator. Jeremiah Cosby believed you got everything you worked for, and the treatment of Bruce went against everything the senator stood for. Unfortunately, those in power at the FBI thought the senator believed in quid pro quo, and everyone believed it was only a matter of when, and not if, the senator was President of the United States.

John was looking at the tuxedo and at Sam. Sam raised an eyebrow.

"So, the senator is going to be there?" John asked. Sam nodded. John reached for the tux. "Are you going to wear that black thing I like?" John was smiling slyly as he asked Sam. Sam smiled at John. John felt his heart melt, the same way he did every time Sam smiled at him. John wished others could be married to their best friend. He couldn't understand how people cut off those they loved.

"Yes, John," Sam answered. "I'm going to wear that 'black thing,'" Sam said, using finger quotes. She shook her head, laughing. "You're one of the greatest detectives the FBI has ever seen, but you can't remember dress names?"

John shrugged, smirking. "If I learn the name, will I get a reward?"

"Out!" Sam pointed toward John's bathroom as she was laughing. John held up his hands and slowly backed out of the door.

"I'm just saying, I have no reason to learn it," John said.

"Out!" Sam shut the door behind John. She turned, leaned up against it, and exhaled a deep breath. She had done it. She had kept it from John. She couldn't remember a time she had ever kept anything from John; him and his stupid ability to notice the body giving away clues. She chuckled to herself. She knew he wouldn't be happy with what the senator was going to propose to him, but it needed to be done. John couldn't keep working by himself; Sam was afraid it was going to get John killed.

Chapter 3

John began to get dressed in his tux as he wondered what it was Sam was trying to keep from him. He wasn't for sure what it was he caught off her, but for some reason, this event was very important to Sam, important enough that she TRIED to keep the reason from him. John tried not to use his "gift," as Sam called it, on Sam. It wasn't fair to her, and John knew it. In his personal life, it had always been a curse. John could always tell when something wasn't right by people's body language. He then began to play over clues in his head until it all connected. Over the years, it had become almost embarrassing some of the things he had figured out. He knew about affairs people were having before their spouses did. He noticed so many things that people just didn't want to get too close to him for fear he'd figure out whatever secret they had, big or small. John couldn't blame them. That was one of the reasons John rarely partnered with anyone.

John tried his best to never "read" Sam, but there were times he just couldn't help himself, especially when it was obvious Sam was trying to hide something. Whatever it was, John was sure it was important to Sam. John and Sam always went through this little dance before John relented when it came to these events, but this time Sam was more determined than ever he go.

John looked in the mirror as he began tying his tie. "You're a lucky man, Mr. Fowler," he said to himself. "Who else would put up with what you do? Who else looks that good in that fancy black thing?"

"I heard that!" Sam yelled through the door. "Thanks," she said, rather shyly.

"Can I come out now?" John asked.

"NO!" Sam yelled. John smiled…and opened the door.

John's Apartment
Now

Chapter 4

"It was a dark and stormy night."

John stared at the words he had typed onto the screen for a few minutes. What had Jeremiah been thinking when he had suggested that he write a book?

"This is why I need a typewriter," he grumbled. "So I can rip this page out and crumple it into a little ball."

John stretched and quickly reached down to grab his chest where the bullet wound continued to heal. He rubbed the spot and got up from the computer desk. John looked around his apartment and thought about how much both it and he had changed in just the past few months. It just seemed like yesterday that Chet had knocked on his door asking him to help the FBI. That case had led to so much.

He had been reunited with his team, Jessica and Chet, and they were once again under the command of Trip. Well, it was supposed to be a one-time thing. John was only supposed to be a consultant on the case. The team had solved what seemed to be a quadruple homicide that turned out to be so much more. John scratched his chin, wondering if anyone else had ever caused the president to resign because of what John had exposed the first lady of being involved in over twenty-five years ago. He shook his head and laughed.

After that, John had been reinstated into the FBI, and his first case was to help his constant nemesis find his kidnapped father. Of course, what John didn't know was his nemesis, Bruce, was the man who had killed his wife and caused him to leave the FBI some three years earlier. During all of this, John had also made up with many of the people he had insulted or distanced himself from during his alcoholism.

John stretched and felt his back pop. Relief spread through his back and shoulders, but not as much relief as he had found tracking down Sam's killer, Bruce. John absentmindedly rubbed the bullet wound he had received from that encounter. John shook his head and laughed. If all of that wasn't enough, Trip and the rest of the team had faked his death. John still wasn't sure that was the best move, but in the end, it helped bring Archibald Staples to justice. And, then, there was the little matter of him getting remarried. John looked down at the ring on his finger and shook his head. His and Jessica's romance had been one of many years and a whirlwind at the same time.

John shook his head and came back to the present. He looked over at the table that was covered in four stacks of folders. They were all FBI cold files. The second biggest stack were cases he was absolutely sure he had solved. The next biggest were the ones that he was 95% sure he had cracked. The small stack that was two files were cases in which he thought he had new leads and had made notes on who to interview next, but had not solved. The big stack on the table were the 60 plus files of the infamous D. B. Cooper case. John grinned. Jessica told him he needed to do something to keep busy during these days he had off to mend; otherwise, he was going to drive her crazy. John turned to the sound of the door opening. Jessica walked in, followed by Chet with three pizzas, Trip holding a case of sodas, and Ron.

"Honey," John said as the group walked in. Chet walked by, perturbed.

"I don't want you asking for any more favors," Chet said as he took the pizzas to the kitchen with Trip following behind him. John turned toward Jessica and Ron.

"He did know I wasn't talking to him?" John asked. "I mean, we're tight and all, but I'm a married man now." Ron smiled, and Jessica rolled her eyes. Jessica gave John a quick peck on the cheek and started in toward the kitchen. Chet walked back into the room.

"I'm not getting you any more files!" Chet exclaimed. "Do you know how many favors I had to pull to get you a copy of the D. B. Cooper case?"

Trip had walked into the kitchen and sat the case of drinks onto the bar beside the pizza. He came back out and looked over the table.

"A little bit of light reading, John?" Trip asked, raising an eyebrow. Jessica walked back to the table.

"Let me see if I can figure these out," she said. Trip nodded for her to go ahead with a bemused look on his face. "This big one here, either these are the ones he solved, or the D. B Cooper case." John pointed toward the big one and mouthed Cooper. Jessica nodded. "So, this one," Jessica said pointing to the smallest on the table, "are the ones he can't quite solve, but has written in the files what the next step should be." Jessica looked at John who nodded. "Finally, this last one, he's only about 95% sure they're solved, but when they're all worked, we'll find out he was right about each of them." Trip whistled appreciatively. Jessica continued. "He just upped your clearance record in about a week." Ron's eyes nearly bugged out of his head.

Chapter 5

"These are all cold cases?" Ron asked. John nodded. "So, you think you've solved 60 or 70?" John took a sip of his drink with one hand and with his other hand pointed up with his thumb. "100?" John bobbed his head around, nodding. Ron and Trip exchanged a look.

Trip ran his hand over his head. "So, what are you going to do with your remaining three weeks of leave?" John held up one finger and tried to look sad. "Three weeks, mandatory. Mess with me, and I'll make it four," Trip stressed. John shrugged. Trip continued. "That's all the cold cases in New York. The rest are in the different offices they originated from, and all the rest from New York are actually in Quantico being changed to digital." John's face fell. Trip had a satisfied smirk as he turned and looked John in the eye. "So, either you solve the D. B Cooper case, or you're going to need to find something else to do." John looked confused. "You see, John, Chet refused to get you anymore cases, and your--," Trip turned toward Jessica, who smiled.

"Roommate who he's married to?" Jessica offered. Trip gave a grimace to the reply. Trip wasn't sure what the rules were on John and Jessica being married and working together, so he chose to believe he knew nothing about it.

"I'll go with roommate," Trip answered.

"That would upset my mother," John said. Trip turned toward John, confused. "She wouldn't like us living in sin."

Trip rolled his eyes. "JESSICA," everyone smiled at his choice of words. Trip continued. "Has threatened anyone who finds something for you to do, and personally, she scares me."

"She scares me too," John said, taking a drink out of his soda bottle. Jessica had walked up to John during the exchange and punched him in the shoulder. "OW!" he exclaimed.

"You big baby," she said as she took the bottle from him and took a drink. John looked at her.

"That was mine," John replied. Jessica stared at him flatly. "But, obviously, I was done with it and wanted you to have the rest." Jessica made a face at John.

"Come on, everyone," she began. "Grab a slice and help yourself to a seat," she said, while motioning toward the couch and chairs in the living room. Chet and Ron headed for the food. Jessica headed back toward the kitchen, and Trip turned to face John.

"Have you given any more thought about writing the book?" Trip asked. John jerked back slightly in surprise.

"Why would I do that?" he asked. "I thought you were just joking, like Jeremiah, when you brought that up. Why would anyone want to read about the things I did?" Trip shrugged.

"I think it would be a pretty interesting read," Trip responded. John stood there, looking at him.

"You're serious?" John asked. Trip nodded. "Where would I even begin?"

"Each story has three parts," Chet answered. Trip, Ron, and John looked at Chet who shrugged. "Sorry, I overheard." John nodded and urged him on. "It doesn't really matter what order you tell the story as long as you tell the beginning, middle, and end."

"No," Trip replied. "See, if you start in the middle, it might confuse people, and then, when you tell the beginning, they think you're just making stuff up because you're out of ideas for what is currently happening, and you're trying to drag things out."

"But, I would be telling what really happened," John replied.

"Doesn't matter," Trip replied. "You would have to do it as fiction because you couldn't tell everything exactly like it happened, so people will think you're just making things up." John thought for a second.

"I mean, I guess I could," John said quietly, sipping on his drink. He caught Jessica looking at him. She had a twinkle in her eyes. John knew where the beginning was; he just wasn't sure everyone was ready to hear it. Besides, what did he know about writing a book? John could hardly turn in case files that passed muster. John looked down at the ground and then back at Trip. "I have been fooling around with something, but I'm not sure everyone wants to hear it," John admitted, looking at Jessica.

"Just write it, John," she said with Trip nodding in agreement. "Let us be the judge of it." John nodded absently. This was about to get interesting.

Chapter 6

A few hours later, after everyone had left, John was in the kitchen, drying the last of the dishes. Jessica was sitting in the living room relaxing, watching someone get their face pounded in on one of those MMA matches. She seemed to be enjoying herself. She had told John to leave the dishes until morning, but John insisted on doing them. He felt he needed to earn his keep since he hadn't been able to work since the shooting. Jessica rolled her eyes and reminded him that he didn't really need to work again. John hadn't really ever thought about that. When his first wife died, the inheritance her grandparents had left her went to John. John had no idea how much money was really in there. When Jessica pressed him on it, he gave her full access to all the accounts and told her to have a look for herself. As far as John was concerned, it was half hers. John had never asked how much was in there after Jessica looked, but she had muttered something about buying her own island.

John had asked her about the two of them retiring, and for a couple of hours, they had actually discussed it. They were watching the news about a young boy that had just been saved from his kidnappers when it hit John that he couldn't leave his job. He loved what he did too much. Honestly, he couldn't leave the puzzles. He turned to Jessica to tell her how he felt, and he saw on her face that she felt the same way. That was the last time they talked about retiring.

The problem was now, John was bored. He was well enough to do things around the house, but at the FBI...well, not yet, and deep down, he knew it.

"Hey, Beagle," Jessica yelled from the living room. "Get in here." John was confused at the name she had called him and wandered into the living room. Jessica was looking up at him with the laptop on her lap.

16

"It was a dark and stormy night?" she asked with a hint of a grin on her face. John shrugged and sat down beside her on the couch. She lay her head on his shoulder but bounced up when one of the fighters caught another in an arm bar and appeared to break his opponent's arm. "That was awesome!" she exclaimed, looking at John. John thought his stomach might heave at the sight.

"That was exactly what I was thinking, awesome," John lied. John felt a hive pop up on his arm and went to scratch it. Jessica frowned at him and laid her head back on his shoulder.

"You big baby," she said. John slightly turned his head to look at her and smiled. Life was comfortable now. Sam's murder was solved. Her killer was in a psychiatric hospital, and John's biggest enemy, Archibald Staples, was in a federal prison, awaiting trial. John knew Archibald had at least two powerful friends that he needed to take down, but for now, things were comfortable.

"Tell the story," Jessica said, never taking her eyes off the TV.

"I'm not sure I can and paint you in a very favorable picture," John replied. Jessica raised her head off John's arm and looked at him. She had a knowing grin on her face.

"Are you saying that in the beginning, I was a bit of trouble?" she asked. John thought for a second. He wanted to choose his words very carefully.

"You were more concerned at times with showing you belonged and could hang with the big boys," he replied. Jessica smiled at him. "And, sometimes, you wanted to make sure we were put in our place." Jessica smiled even more.

"I never thanked you, did I?" Jessica asked. John shrugged. "You could have had me kicked off the team, and no one would have blamed you."

"Sam would have," he replied quietly. Jessica was surprised at that revelation. She hadn't known that and was surprised to hear it. John continued. "I told her what happened. She asked me, given the circumstances, what did I expect a new agent to do." John turned toward Jessica, smiling. "I didn't find out until a few weeks ago exactly how rough that case was on you." Jessica looked confused. "I didn't know you used to live in Knoxville," John said. Jessica smiled broadly.

"Yeah, I guess that did factor in a bit," she conceded. "Write the story, and we'll go from there." She pointed a finger at him, and John kissed the end of it. "You owe me five cents," she said, smiling.

"Only if you have a metal can and do the money dance after I drop the nickel in," John said. Jessica gave him a look.

"I'd call you a stupid beagle, but I don't want to insult beagles," Jessica responded. John threw a pillow at her. The fighters were coming to the ring for the next match, so Jessica laid her head back on John's shoulder to watch the next fight. John watched the fight, but he wasn't really there mentally. He was thinking back to eight years ago. It had all started out so innocently, or so he thought.

FBI Gala
8 Years Ago

Chapter 7

John entered the room, looked around, and groaned to himself. He felt a sharp pain in his shin; he was quite sure that was where Sam had just kicked him to remind him to behave. He glanced at Sam who was smiling at him, broadly. The look in her eyes told him he needed to behave. John smiled back, and the look didn't leave her face. He smiled broader, and Sam barely nodded.

"I feel like a fool," he said, still smiling at people. "I feel like I look like a serial killer or something with this idiotic smile on my face."

"I don't care," Sam replied, her lips never moving. "You are going to behave and act like you're having a good time."

"How do you do that?" John asked, amazed at her not moving her lips while talking to him.

"Years of practice at these things," she replied, still not moving her lips. "Did you understand me? Act like you're having a good time!"

"And, if I don't?" John asked. Sam turned to him, still smiling.

"Don't," she said simply, her lips still never moving. "I'm going to mingle; try not to avoid everyone for the entire night."

"I don't avoid people," he replied. Sam just stared at him for a second.

"Right," she said simply and seemed to just glide off. John watched her go, amazed with her grace. Every time he watched her leave, his heart would still flutter. John turned back toward the party and looked around. His eyes stopped at his friend Chet. John waved, and Chet returned the wave and headed over to him. Chet came over, and the two engaged in small talk for a few seconds. After a minute, Chet turned and stood the same way as John, looking over the crowd.

"Have you seen the new agent?" Chet asked. John closed his eyes and chuckled.

"You seem to forget I'm married," John replied. Chet pursed his lips.

"I didn't say it was a woman or that she was attractive," Chet said defensively. John studied his friend's body language for a second and knew that not only was she female, but she was most attractive. John really wished he understood himself enough to know what he saw in people that told him their secrets. He had spent time with specialists in lying, but they couldn't teach him, and John couldn't teach them. It was very frustrating. John rocked back on his heels and decided to play along.

"Where is she?" John asked.

"I don't know," Chet replied, scanning the crowd. "But, man, when you see her, you'll know who I'm talking about. She is a knockout!"

"Does she use a right hook or a left cross?" came the female voice behind them. John closed his eyes and laughed to himself. If he knew his friend, and he was pretty sure he did, Chet would be so caught up looking for this knockout that he wouldn't realize she was right behind him, talking.

"That's funny," Chet replied, proving John right. "She is absolutely gorgeous." John slightly lowered his head, put his right hand up to his face with his right thumb covering his right cheek, his first two fingers pressed against the middle of his head and his last two fingers cupped under his hand. His left hand came over and took his right elbow. John knew he should get his friend out of trouble, but this was too much fun.

Chapter 8

"I assume you prefer to work with attractive people?" the blond behind John continued. John turned toward her, slightly shaking his head to try to get her to stop giving Chet the rope to hang himself. The blonde shook her head no. It was clear she was enjoying it.

"Well, yeah!" Chet exclaimed and began to turn toward the lady he was talking to. It was then he realized she was the woman he had been scanning the crowd for. John decided it was time to try and save Chet. He extended his hand toward the blonde lady.

"That's a strange name," John began. She gave him a very confused look. "I mean, who names their child Absolutely Gorgeous?" John said with a straight face. She looked at him with shock and a bit of disgust.

"You mean you're actually going to try and cover for him?" she asked. John feigned confusion. She rolled her eyes. "My name is Jessica Hammerstein, and he just called me absolutely gorgeous," she replied with her hands on her hips. John put on his best "ahh" face.

"Now, I get the confusion," John said, turning to Chet. Chet didn't say a word; he had turned a shade of red that John wasn't sure was on the color spectrum. "Her name is Jessica, not Absolutely," John explained to Chet. Chet nodded and scurried off. Jessica began to head after him. John was pretty sure what he was about to do was the wrong move, but he figured in for a penny, in for a pound. He grabbed Jessica's arm as she headed by to stop her. He didn't grab her hard, but the look on her face was anger.

"Who do you think you are?" Jessica said venomously.

"A guy trying to save his friend from getting in trouble with someone who's out to make a name for herself, no matter who she hurts," John replied. Jessica looked like she had been slapped in the face and jerked her arm away from John.

"Now, see here," she began. John knew where this was heading, and he decided to cut it off. He stepped up close to her. Jessica was very shocked and taken aback. John spoke to her very softly, but forcefully.

"I get it," he began. "You've never been appreciated for who you are, and guys, and probably some girls, are always talking about how you got to where you are because of how you look, and you're sick of it. Let me ask you something. Do you think it's worth destroying the career of one of the best computer guys in the history of the FBI because he thinks you look good? Do you think you're going to get anywhere if you're known as the girl who slaps a sexual harassment lawsuit on everyone? Chet was wrong. I'm not defending him, but make the punishment fit the crime, lady. He found you attractive. I bet if you asked him right now, he wouldn't."

Jessica was furious, and she was about to erupt but held in her temper when she saw the man who had invited her to this event. Jeremiah Cosby, with Sam on his arm, walked up to Jessica and John.

"Oh, good," Jeremiah said as he saw the two. "Now, all we need is Chet, and everything will be perfect." John's mind was scrambling. What did the senator know?

"What do you mean?" John asked. Jeremiah smiled broadly like the cat who had eaten the canary.

"Well, you see, John," Jeremiah began. "I want to create a task force and put you in charge of it." John smiled at the idea, but then Jeremiah continued, and the smile fell quickly off John's face. "I want the other two folks I invited to this shindig to be on the task force with you." John's mind was racing. He had a pretty good idea who the other two were, and by the look on Jessica's face, he thought one had been confirmed.

"Who are the other two?" John asked, sick to his stomach.

"Why, Miss Jessica Hammerstein here, and the good Chet Morris," Jeremiah answered proudly. John and Jessica exchanged a look. Then, they looked back at Jeremiah and tried to smile. Sam saw something was wrong, but Jeremiah had noticed nothing and took Sam to find Chet and tell him the good news. John and Jessica stood there for a second.

"Crap," they both said quietly, in unison. They both turned their heads quickly, looking at each other. The waiter came by with drinks, and both grabbed one off the tray. They both gulped their drinks down and glanced at each other.

"I'm going to go find, I don't know, something," Jessica said, pointing aimlessly. John nodded, and Jessica walked off. As she did, John watched her leave and wondered if things could get worse.

"This has to be the worst idea ever," John said to what he thought was himself.

"I agree," came the voice behind him. John turned and saw Lionel Pennyworth Smothers III, or Trip, as he made everyone call him, the Director of the New York office; more importantly, he was John's boss.

"This will never, ever work," Trip said. John had to agree. This was going to be an absolute train wreck. There was no way the three of them could ever work together, ever.

John's Apartment
Now

Chapter 9

John sat at his desk, staring at the words he had typed. He glanced at the clock and saw that it was after 2 am. John ran his hand through his hair. This writing stuff was harder than he thought it was going to be. He had teared up a couple of times, thinking about that night so long ago. John loved his new life, but some nights, he missed Sam. John glanced out the window, trying to shake the thoughts of long ago from his head. The night skyline was absolutely breathtaking. Sam had loved the skyline.

John got up, walked over to the window, and looked out. He looked down at the sidewalk and took a step back in surprise at the person he saw on the sidewalk. The figure he saw was Sam; he was sure of it. He wiped his eyes in shock. He and Jessica had seen his wife a couple of times since her death. They had both originally written it off to their subconscious seeing her to deal with her death. Over the past few weeks, he and Jessica had discussed it. Jessica had begun to wonder if it was because of the promise that she and Sam had made when they were both alive that if one of them died first, that person would watch over the other like a guardian angel.

John took a second look at where he thought he had seen Sam. On second glance, he realized no one was there, but someone that resembled Sam turned the corner and disappeared into the alleyway down the street. John wasn't for sure what he had seen, but this was different. Usually if he saw Sam, she made herself known to him.

John scratched his head in confusion, shrugged, and wandered into the bedroom. Jessica was in bed asleep.

John was pretty sure she'd inflict physical damage to him if he woke her to tell her what he had seen. John shrugged, climbed into bed, and stared at the ceiling. Even when things had been going well for him, John only slept six to seven hours a night at best. His mind was always running, thinking about things he had seen that day. Some of his biggest breaks in cases had been while he lay in bed, thinking about something he observed that day.

Early on in his marriage to Sam, she used to get upset when he would spring from the bed. Within a few months, Sam only got upset if John woke her up to tell her something about the case that could have waited until morning. When John got up, he would pace the living room, studying his board he had created at home until the case broke, or he figured out his next move. In fact, there were some cases when he just didn't sleep. Toward the end of his time undercover, John probably drank more hours a day than he would sleep.

Since he had been shot, John would do good to sleep four hours a night and nap for a couple of hours during the day. He hadn't told Jessica, but the naps were just about nonexistent currently, and he wasn't averaging more than three or four hours a night. Jessica seemed oblivious to it all. Once she went to bed, she usually didn't wake up. That was why he was very surprised when her voice cut through the night.

"You're in bed early," Jessica said, causing John to jump. She rolled over and smiled at him.

"Came to a good stopping point," he replied. Jessica put her elbow on the pillow, pushed up, and placed her head in her hand, looking at him.

"What's wrong?" she asked quietly. John looked over at her and then back at the ceiling. He figured it probably wasn't best to start off a marriage telling lies, especially to someone who used the least little excuse to practice the jiu-jitsu moves she had learned.

"I saw Sam, but it didn't look like her, and instead of disappearing like she's done in the past, she walked down the street," John said, waiting for Jessica to make fun of him. She didn't and was very quiet. John looked over at her, and Jessica had on what John called her considering face. John didn't try to read her, but not reading people for John was like not breathing for anyone else. Jessica was considering telling him something that might upset him was the best way John knew how to describe it. "What is it?"

"I thought I saw her on our wedding day. We were at the graveyard when I thought I saw her, but when I looked away, she had disappeared. We walked a little ways, and Sam was standing by a tree. She talked to me a minute and then told me it wasn't her I saw when I asked her why she had also shown herself to me on the other side of the graveyard," Jessica was quiet. John waited. He knew she wasn't done. Jessica continued even more quietly. "She said to tell you it's not her fault." John sat up quickly, looking at Jessica.

"Why didn't you tell me about this earlier?" John asked. Jessica raised an eyebrow.

"Why didn't I tell you on our wedding day that your dead wife gave me a message to give you about someone who appears to look like her?" Jessica asked. John bobbed his head, considering what she said.

"Well, when you put it that way," he conceded. Jessica gave him a look that told him he was an idiot for even having to ask the question to start with. John thought for a second and decided to ask the question that had been floating around in his head for the past few months anytime either of them had seen Sam. "Are we crazy?" John asked, looking back at Jessica. She knew exactly what John meant, and with the latest instances of seeing Sam, Jessica wasn't so sure she knew the answer any longer. Jessica shook her head, not knowing the answer.

"I don't know, John. I just don't know."

Chapter 10

A few blocks away, Amanda entered an all-night café she had been in numerous times in the past few weeks. Amanda sat down at a booth and ordered a vanilla milkshake. It was just far enough away from her destination that her target wouldn't see her.

Amanda looked down at her shaking hand. She had messed up, and she knew it. She wasn't supposed to let John see her. The plan was for her to observe only. She had been seen twice, once by him and once by the tramp he had just married. She thought about calling her father but knew exactly what he would say. "You've made a mistake. Now, do what you can to make the most out of it."

How could she use this mistake to her advantage? More importantly, when did that man sleep? Amanda sat staring at the napkin dispenser, trying to think of a way to correct this problem. A slow smile started to form on her face. What if she did let him get glimpses of her? What if she let him think that maybe, just maybe, Samantha was alive? She paused for a second. Did he call her Samantha, or that crude, common name, Sam? That would be just like him to take something so beautiful and wonderful and sully it. Her father had warned her that was the kind of man John Fowler was, crude and classless.

Her milkshake came, and she smiled. Her mother had loved vanilla milkshakes, at least that's what her father had told her. Amanda had never drank any other type but vanilla. It was one of the many things she did to honor her mother the way her father had taught her. Her father always told her she was as beautiful as her mother. She had done everything she could to remind her father of the beauty of her mother. It was the least she could do, since she was the daughter of one of the greatest men in the history of the world. She would remind John Fowler of exactly how great a man her father was. That's what she was going to do to John, just before she killed him.

Kenneth Nichols, Washington, D.C.
Now

Chapter 11

Kenneth sat at his desk, working the phone. He was trying every trick he knew to free Archibald. His friend, and associate, had been arrested because of the screw-up of his father. Kenneth really hated when people were incompetent, especially his father. He hung up the phone and leaned back in his chair. He wondered what his daughter was doing. He chuckled to himself as he thought back to the conversation he and Archibald had several years ago.

Archibald was the only person besides his father that knew exactly who Amanda was. Archibald had arrived at Kenneth's safe house one day. Amanda had shown Archibald in. Archibald couldn't get over how much she looked and acted like her mother. Amanda had left the two men to discuss business. Archibald had turned to Kenneth, and Kenneth could easily read the concern on Archibald's face.

"What is it?" Kenneth asked. Archibald looked a little uncomfortable.

"Well, I don't want you to take this the wrong way, but she acts exactly like Samantha," Archibald said. Kenneth nodded, not seeing any problem. Archibald chose his words carefully and continued. "Some might wonder with the past you had with her mother…" Archibald trailed off, not sure how to continue. Kenneth suddenly understood.

"Are you asking me if I have had an inappropriate relationship with my daughter?" Kenneth asked. Archibald shrugged and looked toward the doorway that Amanda had left through. "Archibald," Kenneth began. "I'm a man who believes in family values." Archibald nearly spit his drink out, and both men roared with laughter. Kenneth chuckled and then turned deadly serious.

"Don't you see the beauty of it Archibald?" Kenneth asked. "If anything unfortunate ever happened to my beloved, then I would have the perfect weapon to drive her worthless husband mad." A sick, evil smile covered Kenneth's face. "There's nothing inappropriate going on between me and my daughter. I'm just teaching her how to kill the man who took her mother from us. Maybe one day I can rid the world of John Fowler and reunite my family, the way it was meant to be." Archibald smiled. Most fathers would be mad knowing that their sons-in-law would speak openly about leaving their daughters for another woman, but most fathers weren't Archibald. He knew that Kenneth had an unnatural obsession with destroying John Fowler and getting back what Kenneth believed was the love of his life, Samantha. The irony was that John Fowler didn't even really know that Kenneth hated everything associated with him.

Kenneth let the memories go and thought about the present. Very soon, he would free his friend, and his daughter would finish off John. Life wasn't great right now, but it would be again very, very soon.

Chapter 12

John lay in bed and stared at the ceiling, his mind racing. Jessica was lying beside him doing the same. It was late, or early, depending on how you looked at time. It was 3:00 a.m., and Jessica knew she wasn't sleeping for a while with these thoughts in her head.

"Come on," she said, throwing off the covers. "Neither one of us is going to get any kind of sleep like this." She took off down the hall, and John decided he should follow. He walked into the living room and put his hand over his eyes when Jessica flipped the light on. She had a glass of water and handed him one. She sat down on the couch, put her glass on the coffee table, and patted the spot beside her for him to sit down.

"What are we doing?" he asked, sitting beside her.

"We're going to figure this out like two trained investigators," she replied.

"Then, we're going to the loony bin because we're both seeing a dead woman," John replied, taking a sip of his water after speaking. Jessica pressed her lips together, blew her cheeks out, and nodded slightly.

"Okay, then we're going to figure out who this person is we're seeing," Jessica replied. John looked at her, confused.

"It's my dead wife, your dead friend, Sam," John responded like she was an idiot.

"John," Jessica said sharply.

"Sorry," he replied.

"Did you see Sam tonight? Because whoever it was I saw the other day, it wasn't Sam," Jessica stressed.

33

"Are you sure?" John asked. Jessica sighed. She wasn't sure. It really resembled Sam, but she didn't think it was.

"I'm pretty sure," Jessica said.

"And, what do we know about eyewitnesses?" John asked. Jessica punched the cushion in frustration, causing John to jump in surprise.

"Enough!" she exclaimed. "Sam is dead; that is one thing we both know. Another thing we both know is we both see someone who claims she is her, and whether you want to admit it or not, I know in my heart it's Sam. The question is who is this other person?" John was staring down at the floor.

"The person who said she is Sam, is Sam," John responded quietly. "I know it is. I just don't know how." Jessica reached over and took his hands, and John looked at her.

"Okay," Jessica said softly. "Then, who is this other person?"

"I have no idea," John replied.

"Is it Sam?" Jessica asked. John started to respond, but Jessica stopped him. "Close your eyes and think. Is it her?" John shut his eyes, opened them, and looked at Jessica.

"This is weird," John said. Jessica gave him a level look. John loved Jessica, but sometimes she scared him a little, and this was one of those times. "But, I do believe in trying new, weird things," John responded quickly as he shut his eyes. "Since I've gotten remarried," he added under his breath. Jessica playfully punched him in the arm. John shut his eyes and concentrated. He could see the person that was watching the apartment, but she was far away, and he only got a glimpse of her. The shape of her face was Sam's, but it wasn't. The hair was definitely Sam's; the height, it was slightly off. Why hadn't he

34

noticed it before? It was an inch or so difference. No, that wasn't possible. John couldn't tell that from upstairs looking out his window, could he? He concentrated more.

There was something about the girl that screamed Sam, but it wasn't natural. It was like it was taught. It was like she was playing a part. Her walk and her gait, they weren't natural, but they were Sam's. What did that mean? His eyes flew open, and he looked at Jessica who had a knowing look on her face. "How did you know I could do that?" he asked. Jessica had a satisfied smile on her face.

"I've speculated on it for years after Sam told me about your nightly roamings," she replied. "It only made sense that when you were up walking around and making conclusions, it was always something you saw earlier that day. I've always thought that somehow, you can see things like a camera in your mind. I don't know for sure, but I'm guessing you can zoom in, zoom out, or replay scenes in your mind." From the look on John's face, Jessica was sure she was right. "What did you see?" John shook his head speculatively but continued on when Jessica gave him a leveled look.

"Her face was Sam's, but it wasn't," John said. Jessica raised an eyebrow but encouraged him on. "And I can't tell you how I know this, but I think she was taller than Sam. There's something else. Everything else seems to be Sam, but it's not. It's like it's taught."

"So, what does that mean?" Jessica asked, very excited. John looked at her with an expression she hadn't seen for some time. It was the look John had when he didn't have an answer and didn't even know where to start to find one. The last time she had seen that look was over Sam's death.

"I have no idea," John admitted.

35

Chapter 13

"What do you mean you have no idea?" Jessica asked, her face incredulous. John shook his head, looking defeated. Jessica shook her head. "I refuse to accept that answer," she said. John leaned back, amusement covered his face.

"It's not that simple, Jess," John answered. Jessica grabbed his jaw between her thumb and first finger and held it tightly.

"Listen to me," she began, very quietly and intensely. "You solved numerous cold cases with less. This is where your problem lies. Anything that bothers you emotionally, you shut down. This has to do with Sam, and that hurts you inside, I get it, but we have to figure this out. Do you understand? We are part of a major task force within the FBI with ties to Homeland Security. If word gets out the two of us are seeing your dead wife, do you know what will happen?"

John managed to nod his head with Jessica holding his jaw. Jessica was staring intently at John, not blinking. John was beginning to wonder if she was ever going to let go of his jaw.

"Here's the deal, John. If you don't figure this out, you can't go back to the FBI because I will tell Trip what we are seeing," Jessica stated, looking scared. "Do you understand what that means? If you don't solve this, both of us--not just you--but both of us, are gone from the FBI. Do you understand that?" John nodded, and Jessica let go of his jaw. John rubbed his jaw and looked at Jessica, confused.

"Why does this matter?" John asked.

"Because someone is out there making me think my friend might still be alive, and I'm married to her widower," Jessica responded, tears welling in her eyes and her voice wavering. John looked down at the ground.

"Oh," he responded. He thought for a second about all that implied. If Sam were alive, then he and Jessica... His eyes widen, and he turned back to Jessica. "OH!" he exclaimed, putting it all together. Jessica nodded, tears in her eyes. John moved close, putting his right hand on her cheek.

"Is this about me picking her over you?" John asked. Jessica shook her head with tears in her eyes. "I really shouldn't believe you, should I?" John asked. Jessica looked at him and slightly shook her head. "Do you think she's alive?" Jessica shook her head no. "Are you afraid she's alive?" Jessica burst out into tears. John didn't really know what to do. He held her which was probably his best choice.

"I want her to be alive, John. I do, but how is it possible?" Jessica said.

"Jess, she's dead," John replied as carefully as he could. Jessica looked up into his eyes. "This isn't the movies, or a soap opera, or a comic book, or anything like that. She's dead." Jessica nodded.

"I know, John," she replied. "But, deep down, I want her to be alive, but if she is..." Jessica couldn't continue.

"She's not," John said, thinking that was the end of it. Jessica gave John a look to let him know he was wrong again. John sighed. "I'll never understand, will I?" John asked. Jessica snorted a laugh and gently pushed herself away from John.

"No," she replied, running her right hand down his cheek. "You never will. And, I honestly don't expect you to," she added. John nodded. "But, you have to figure this out because I am going to hurt whoever is doing this to us." John wanted to tell her it wasn't bothering her nearly as bad as it was bothering him, but he thought better of it. He really wanted to go back to the FBI, and he knew she was serious. John had to figure out who this person was. That shouldn't be too big of a problem. He was an FBI agent after all. The good news was at least he could quit writing the book. A smile began to form on his face.

"One more thing," she added, putting the tip of her finger on his chest. John looked at her, smiling. "You have to finish the book." The smile fell off his face.

Chapter 14

John and Jessica talked for a few more minutes, and Jessica decided she was going back to bed. John walked in two minutes later and Jessica was sound asleep. John lay down, and sleep came quickly. Daylight poured in the window when he opened his eyes. Jessica had already left for work, and he was all alone in the apartment. John didn't know what to do about finding the person who looked like Sam, but he had an idea. John rolled out of bed and made a phone call. The person on the other end sounded quite surprised but agreed to meet John at his apartment. John took a shower, got dressed, and waited for his guest.

There was a knock on the door, and John answered. John let Ronald McGuire, who was still somewhat surprised about being asked to help, inside.

"John," Ronald began. "I appreciate the call, but I'm a little surprised. I would have thought you would have wanted Chet for this."

"Because he and I have known each other for so long?" John asked, showing Ron to the couch. Ron took a seat and nodded at John's question. "The lack of involvement in this case is exactly why I want you to help me." Ron still looked confused. "Jessica and I are way too close to what is going on. Chet, on the other hand, won't be able to tell me the truth if I am seeing things. I need you to be honest, something you seem to have no trouble doing." Ron nodded. He looked around the room as if thinking of what to say. John got up and got a bottle of water. He offered Ron one who politely declined. John walked back to his chair and sat down. "Either way this works out, I'll owe you one. I'll help you on whatever case it is that is bothering you."

Ron snapped his head around quickly. The look on his face was incredulous. "How?" he asked simply. John chuckled.

"It's what I do," John replied mysteriously. He then burst into laughter. Ron looked a little irritated. John held his hand up as if to say, "wait." "I figure you have a reason for asking everyone in the world to be in the New York office, and then when you wanted to be made a permanent member, I knew something was up. I mean, come on, you guys in Delta Force don't just come to the FBI. You're after something, and you've never denied that." Ron nodded.

"I never said I was in Delta Force," Ron said quietly. John just looked at Ron. "Don't you want to know what I'm after?" Ron asked. John shook his head.

"When you're ready for me, you'll tell me, simple as that," John replied. "I'm sure it's on the level. Everything you've ever done has been." John got up and headed toward the kitchen to make himself some breakfast. Ron's gut churned. Had that been a dig, or did John know? Ron used every technique he had studied since learning about John's ability to not give anything away. Satisfied that he had control of himself, Ron got up and headed for the door.

"You want to know whatever I find out?" Ron asked. John nodded. "Be careful what you ask for," Ron warned and left the apartment. John nodded. Something was slightly off with Ron at the end, but John chalked it up to Ron's excitement about the case in which John offered to help. John turned toward the computer and stared at it. He knew Jessica was serious about him writing a book. He wasn't sure, but he thought she had decided it was some kind of therapy for him.

"I guess it's time," he said to the machine. "How do people do this for a living?"

Chapter 15

A few hours later, Jessica walked up to the door of her apartment she now shared with John, her new home. She couldn't help but smile. She never thought the two of them would be together, much less married. The smile on her face changed to surprise as she heard music coming through the door. It was an 80s song, as usual, but this one…this one was one that somewhat surprised Jessica. She couldn't remember the name of the song or the band. The female lead singer's name was on the tip of her tongue. What surprised Jessica was that John was listening to what he would call a suggestive song.

Jessica didn't really think of John as a prude, although most would. John just lived by a very different code than most people, a code of an ancient ninja race that no one knew the doctrine of but him. Shaking her head, Jessica let herself in. She opened the door and was even more surprised. The music was blaring, something John never did, but even more surprising than that, John was swaying his hips to the music while washing dishes. He was using a spatula sporadically as an imaginary microphone. Jessica sat her things down and quietly shut the door. She dug through her purse and found a dollar. She entered the kitchen area, and John saw her. Instead of stopping, he continued to sing and began to sing to her. She held up the dollar with a big smile on her face, folded it, and slipped it into the waistband of his jeans. John laughed out loud.

"This one's free, ma'am," John said, smiling. Jessica was shaking her head.

"What has gotten into you?" she asked.

"I've finished the next part of the book, and I'm just glad to be done with it," John answered. Jessica tried to think what would have come next in the story. Her face reddened a bit, and John grinned.

"Would that be," she began and stopped as John nodded with his annoying smirk on his face. She shook her head. The music continued on a loop, and John began dancing again. She laughed.

"What brings you home?" he asked, still dancing. Jessica put her arms around his shoulders and attempted to dance with him. He was slightly off-beat.

"My boss thought I should spend some quality time with my husband, and I thought that was a good idea," she responded.

"Would this be the same boss that really doesn't want to know that you're married?" John asked. Jessica laughed and pulled John closer.

"The same," she replied. John had that irritating smirk on his face.

"Are you going to read what I wrote?" John asked. Jessica nodded and leaned in toward John. John stopped dancing.

"Later," she responded very quietly and kissed John. "Much later."

FBI Gala
8 Years Ago

Chapter 16

John got away from Trip without having to talk to him too much. He liked Trip, but the man was so uptight and by the book. "By the Book Lionel," was the name he had been given in the office. John thought he would have narced on George Washington if he hadn't have come clean about the cherry tree. John made his way through the crowd and found his wife, sans Jeremiah. She saw him and made a beeline toward him.

"What did you do?" she asked, not bothering to try and be quiet.

"Why do you think it's always me?" John asked, a little put off by the question. Sam put her hands on her hips and gave him that look. The look was the one all guys get when they know what they've done is wrong, but they try to lie, cover something up, or act innocent when they're not. "Honestly," he continued. "I didn't really do anything. It was mostly Chet's fault." John winced as soon as he said it. He had just thrown Chet under the bus, and he was really afraid there might be no saving him. Of course, Chet didn't have to live with Sam, so better Chet than him.

"What did you two do?" Sam asked, much more sternly this time. John looked around, hoping for anything that might be going on that he could use as an excuse to tell her. Where were armed lunatics when you needed them? "John!" she said quietly but with her teeth clenched. At that point, John knew he was in for it. He quickly spewed out everything. As he watched his wife's face, it went from humor to horror. When he finished, Sam looked as though she had a migraine.

"You two idiots realize you may have just ruined Senator Cosby's big moment, right?" she asked, clearly very irritated.

"I didn't do anything," John insisted.

"That's the problem!" Sam exclaimed, quietly but fiercely. "Why didn't you stop him before he got on one of his rolls? We've talked about this, John. You two can't just say what you want like you can when the two of you are in your cubes at the office. People don't know how to take the two of you when you get going!"

"Well, it's better this happened now before she ended up on our team and got me or Chet in trouble," John said, looking around for the senator. John missed the look of shock and horror on Sam's face. She reached up, grabbed his jaw, and whipped his head toward her so he wouldn't miss anything.

"Don't you dare blame her for this!" she said. John gulped. "Whether or not Chet meant anything by it doesn't matter. What matters is how she took it, and you two have got to make it right."

"I didn't do anything," John almost whimpered. Sam just stared at him. John had been married long enough to understand what had just happened. He sighed, defeated.

Chapter 17

John wandered off to find Chet or Jessica. He saw Jessica, and she saw him. He started toward her, and she attempted to avoid him. After a minute or so, he finally caught up to her.

"I didn't see you there," Jessica said, knowing he had seen her. An unpleasant smile was on her face. John stuck his hands in his pockets and looked down at the floor and wondered how mad Sam would be if he didn't fix this. He glanced over to where she had been and saw her. He turned back to what he figured was the lesser of two evils, took a deep breath, and began.

"I apologize for my and my friend's actions," John said. "It was insensitive, and I will take all repercussions that I deserve. I was serious earlier about my friend. He never meant anything by it, and I would hate to see his career ruined."

Jessica was a little surprised by John's words, and a satisfied smile crossed her face.

"Any repercussions?" she asked. John nodded. "Verbalize," she said. John clenched his jaw. Jessica had a challenging look on her face. John could tell he was never going to get along with this woman. He felt sorry for whatever guy that had the misfortune to date or, God forbid, marry her.

"Anything," he said.

"I want on the team," she said. John's stomach fell to his feet. He thought things couldn't get any worse. "I also want the two of you to take the sexual harassment course." John was obviously wrong. It could get worse. The question was how much worse? "Take the course, both of you, and both of you accept me on the team, and I won't report the earlier incident. Deal?" She held out her hand.

"You realize the training is two days?" John asked.

"Oh, I do," she replied, a satisfied smirk crossing her face. She looked down at her hand and back at him. "Deal?" John, looking defeated, reached out and took her hand. As soon as he did, a smirk crossed his face. The smirk screamed that he knew something that she didn't. Jessica instantly could tell with the look on his face that he felt he had somehow won. He shook her hand.

"Deal," he said. He let go of her hand and tried to turn, but he noticed she hadn't let go of his hand. The look on her face caused his smirk to grow even more. "Oh," he said. "I didn't tell you that Trip had offered Chet and me two additional vacation days to give us incentive to attend the training. As I promised, neither of us will oppose you joining the team." Disgusted, Jessica threw his hand down and stormed off. John, whistling tunelessly, walked back over to Sam who had been observing the whole thing.

"I'm assuming that was her?" she asked. John, very proud of himself, nodded. He was missing the signs she was giving off; the signs any married man knows whether they had John's gift or not. "You like her," Sam said smiling, taking a sip of her drink. John looked stunned. He slowly turned towards her.

"Her?" he asked, jerking his thumb in Jessica's direction. Sam nodded, enjoying his reaction. "I can't stand her."

"Mm-hmm," she replied, just looking at John. John shook his head.

"What makes you think I like her?" he asked, still baffled. "She's full of herself. She's got an insecurity complex unlike any I've ever seen."

"Look in the mirror," Sam interjected. John ignored her and continued.

"And, she thinks she's all that," John finished.

"All that?" Sam asked. John nodded.

"All that," he replied. Sam sighed.

"We've talked about this, John," Sam said. "You should not repeat things you hear on movies or TV. It just doesn't sound right coming from you." Sam started to head to their table. John started to make a point as she walked away, and again, he was caught in mid-gesture. He made a face and followed her.

"Why do you do that?" he asked. Sam stopped, turned, and took his head in her hands.

"Do what?" she asked innocently.

"Walk off just as I'm starting to make my point," he replied.

"Because first, you have no real point, and second, if I don't keep you off balance, you'll get too full of yourself," she replied smiling.

"We wouldn't want that now, would we?" John said, the smirk beginning to cross his face. Sam shook her head quickly, smiling.

"Down, Tiger," she said softly. She took his hand and led him to his seat.

Chapter 18

John sat through dinner, miserable. It was everything John despised. John hated formal attire and being forced to dress up, which was ironic since he had to wear a suit every day in the FBI. The night was pure torture. He knew every time someone lied at the table just to make himself sound important. He was exhausted with all of the observation. All John wanted to do was sit in a room, by himself--well with Sam would be alright--listening to music or in complete silence and decompress. However, there was no way that was happening for at least a few hours. John thought the food would be good when he was told it was to be chicken, but it was dry. There was asparagus as a side (who eats asparagus?), and what he thought was mashed potatoes were actually mashed sweet potatoes. John mumbled under his breath until Sam kicked him in the shin.

The only part of the dinner John enjoyed was Jessica glaring at him. He picked up a fork full of chicken, raised it to her, and took a bite with a big smile on his face while he chewed. Sam leaned over to him as Jessica stared daggers through him.

"I don't read people like you do, but I think she hopes you choke," Sam said without moving her lips.

"MMM-HMM." John replied, still smiling. Jessica looked even angrier.

"Why are you making her mad?" Sam asked.

"I find I enjoy it," John replied. Jessica set her jaw and didn't look amused.

"I think you're flirting," Sam said while taking a bite of her chicken. John nearly spit the food out of his mouth. He turned toward Sam with a look of shock on his face. He noticed the small smile that now was on Jessica's face. That irritated him, but there was nothing he could do about it at the moment.

"Why would you think I would ever flirt with her?" John asked as quietly as he could. John felt, more than saw, Jessica chuckling. Sam had a knowing smile on her face.

"John," she began. "I don't think you would ever do a thing with her, ever. However, there's something about her that you like. There's nothing wrong with that. You can just never ever act on it. You're mine, Mr. Fowler. Never forget that." John looked into her eyes and saw something that he wasn't sure he had ever seen before. He picked up a napkin and wiped around his mouth, never taking his eyes off her.

"She's off the team," John said. Sam shook her head and gave John a look. John felt his stomach drop. This wasn't over like he thought.

"Tell me about her," Sam said.

Chapter 19

"What's there to tell?" he asked. "She's supposedly the best there is at interrogation. She's known to have a temper about her, which I personally witnessed, and she's supposedly on the fast track to being the big boss one day if she can curb her attitude."

"What attitude?" Sam asked.

"She thinks that everyone thinks she got where she is because of her looks and her taking advantage of it," John replied. The look on Sam's face made John involuntarily gulp.

"Is there any proof of it?" Sam asked.

"None that I know of," John said, taking a drink of water. He felt like he was being interrogated.

"Do you trust her?" Sam asked, her eyes sparkling dangerously. John wasn't sure where this was going.

"Huh?" he asked.

"Do. You. Trust. Her?" she asked again.

"From what I can tell, she's like a bulldog," John answered. "I'd probably fight with her as much as an enemy, but she's someone you'd want in a foxhole with you. Honestly, besides Chet, there's probably no one I'd rather go to war with than her. She'll either be one of the greatest here, or she'll flame out in two years because of her attitude."

"So, you're telling me the only chance this girl has is to be on your team?" Sam asked. John thought about it for a second. He rubbed his tongue along the inside of his lower jaw. He had a bad feeling he had just been outflanked. He could see no way out of the situation he found himself in. John looked at Sam and barely nodded. He was her only hope, he knew that, but he couldn't work with her, not if Sam thought he was flirting with her.

"So, you're telling me you're going to give up on her because of something that's not her fault?" she asked.

John knew where this was going. He didn't know what it was in her past that had happened, but whenever someone was judged based on what others saw, instead of the actual truth, then Sam became their champion. John knew he had to get control of this before it was too late.

"Now, look," John began. Sam held up a hand. John noticed Jessica with her hand over her mouth to cover her laughing. This was not going well.

"Now, you look, mister," Sam countered. John groaned internally. He had rather face an army of bank robbers all carrying automatic weapons with him only having a sling shot and no rocks than hear one of Sam's, "now you look here mister." John was done for, and he knew it. "All she is doing is trying to be the best agent she is, and she is being judged unfairly. Just because you've got a thing for her--"

"Thing!?" John interjected. Sam ignored him and plowed right on.

"Is not her fault," she continued, her eyes dancing. John couldn't help but smile. He loved how Sam fought for people. She had a heart that was immeasurable. "She can't help it that something about her excites something in you."

"Excites?" John repeated, flabbergasted. Sam pinched his nose. Jessica nearly choked on her food when she saw that. John wondered what she would say, or do, if she knew that she was the topic of conversation.

"She remains on the team," Sam said. "I trust you, John."

"I don't even like the girl," John said, defeated.

"Of course, dear," Sam replied, running her hand through his hair. John sighed. He was beat, and he knew it.

Chapter 20

"She deserves a chance, John," Sam told him, holding his hands. John nodded. He knew she did. It was just going to be hard. He and Chet worked on a lot of things together. They weren't partners, but they were close. The senator appeared beside the two.

"May I interrupt you two lovebirds?" the senator asked. Sam and John both smiled at him. "Could I ask this pretty young thing for a dance?"

"Be my guest, sir," John replied. Sam smiled at John, and John saw something in the smile to let him know he was about to be set up. His eyes widened as he tried to shake his head no.

"Jessica," Sam called across the table. Jessica looked at Sam.

"The senator has asked me to dance," she began. "John will just sit here the rest of the night if someone doesn't force him onto the dance floor. He's not very good, but his therapist says it helps him open up if someone will dance with him. Can I be a bother and ask you to help him?"

"Therapist?" John mouthed at Sam with a confused look on his face. Sam ignored him, but a smile flickered on the corners of her mouth. "Therapist?" John mouthed to the senator. The senator just shrugged, but the smile on his face told John that he was enjoying watching John being set up. John turned toward Jessica just knowing she would say no. His heart sank when he saw the mischievous look on her face.

"He can't dance?" she asked Sam.

"Not a lick," Sam replied.

"You've got it," Jessica replied. Sam and the senator headed toward the dance floor. "I guess you got your orders," she said to John, clearly enjoying herself.

"You have no idea," John replied, watching his wife and the senator on the dance floor. John's mind was wheeling. This team was all Sam's idea; he was sure now. He didn't know how many times she had talked about how she wanted someone John trusted to watch his back. She worried about him more than was necessary, John thought, but she did worry. John looked over at Jessica who was watching everyone else. She was clearly thinking about something, and it seemed she had come to a conclusion. She turned to John.

"Have I done something wrong?" she asked. John was a little surprised.

"Why would you ask that?" John asked.

"You don't like me," she began. John started to reply, but Jessica held up her hand. "I know how I can come off, and while it's not right, it's not right the way I'm treated." John nodded.

"I've never been great at speaking," John began. Jessica snorted and tried to hold in a chuckle. John gave her a level look, and Jessica managed to reel in some of her laughter. John continued. "I can never say I know what it's like being accused of the things you have attained because of how you look. I've never had that problem." Jessica gave a slight smile, and John couldn't help but grin. "However, I can tell you what my boneheaded friend said, he said as a compliment. That being said, if it offended you in any way I know he is sorry and would tell you himself, but he is scared of you. Scared of your beauty, your reputation, and your ability to get him fired. If I offended you, then I am sorry. Men, for the most part, say what comes to their minds without thinking. That's not to say it's okay. It's just the truth. If you'd like, we can go to human resources on Monday, you can file a complaint about me, and I will gladly sign it and pay whatever consequences that are appropriate." John looked over at

Jessica and was surprised he was having trouble reading her. He wasn't trying to get out of trouble. He was trying to be honest and build the beginnings of a working relationship.

"It was no big deal," Jessica said quietly. "I just want to be accepted."

"Then, work with me and Chet," John said. "Not because you have to, but because we can show you how to do things the right way, and no one, and I mean no one, can question your career advancement." John held his hand out. Jessica gave him a strange look. She smiled, nodded, and shook his hand. John started to pull his hand away, but Jessica held on to it.

"I still have to do the training," John said, clearly not happy. Jessica nodded, and John tried to pull his hand away, but she stopped it again. "Keep it up, and I'll be lodging a complaint," John quipped. Jessica smiled.

"I need you to be brutally honest with me about everything," Jessica said. John slowly nodded.

"Remember, you asked for it," he replied. Jessica dropped his hand, stood up, and looked at the dance floor and then back at John. John shook his head. She looked over at Sam and then back at John.

"You wouldn't?" he asked. The look of pleasure on Jessica's face told him she would. John got to his feet, grumbling, and headed to the dance floor with Jessica. How did he always find himself in these situations? Where was a nut with a bomb when you needed one?

Chapter 21

As John stepped onto the dance floor, he noticed several agents grabbing their ringing cell phones. John wondered how long it was going to be until he was forced to carry his cell phone. Trip was heading his way with a purpose.

"Some nut has a bomb," Trip said. "He's been arrested, but the senator reminded me of your new task force, so it looks like this is your first case."

"Anyone hurt?" John asked. Trip shook his head no, and John said a quick prayer of thanks, both for no one being hurt and for getting him out of this dancing mess. Trip turned to leave, and John started after him. John remembered that Jessica was now on the team, and turned toward Jessica.

"You know," she began. "Some men would kill to dance with me. You seem to go out of your way not to."

"Some men are idiots," John replied and then silently cursed himself. "Look, that came out wrong," he tried to explain. Jessica was smiling.

"For someone who's supposed to be one of the greatest minds at the FBI, you sure do some dumb things," Jessica said, smiling. John thought about protesting, knowing she had taken what he said the wrong way. He gathered himself and then calmly explained.

"I have this problem of seeing things in black and white, and sometimes, I speak that way," John explained. "While you're a lovely lady, and I mean that in the most complimentary, non-discriminatory way, a man would be an idiot to kill someone just to dance with you." Jessica just shook her head and headed after Trip. John stood there a second after she walked by.

"Well," he said to no one. "That went well." John didn't notice Sam coming up behind him.

"Are you going with them?" Sam asked. John turned toward her.

"I'm afraid I've got to," John said, taking her hand and preparing an apology in his head. Sam smiled which threw him.

"Great," she said, confusing John. "I can't wait to see this team in action."

John shook his head, smiling.

"You're proud of yourself on this, aren't you?" he asked. Sam smiled and nodded.

"I think I've out done myself this time," she replied. "Now get," she said, pointing toward the door. "You know you have no want to be here." John smiled and moved in close to her.

"Have I told you how lucky I am to have you in my life?" he asked. Sam's smile could have lit up the entire room.

"Not lately," she quipped. John smiled, kissed her, and hurried off with Chet in tow. The senator came up beside her.

"Are you sure about this?" he asked her. Sam turned toward the senator and smiled.

"Nope," she replied. "But, I've got to do something, or he's going to come back dead, or worse." The senator looked at her in disbelief.

"Mah dear," the senator began. "What in tarnation could be worse than death?"

"With John, you just never know," Sam replied. "You just never know."

Bruce Cosby
Now

Chapter 22

Bruce lifted his head from the book he was reading. He saw the attendant approaching his room. Bruce looked around and chuckled. You really couldn't call it a room. It truly was a prison cell, just bigger than most cells, and located in a psychiatric hospital. Bruce wasn't insane, that he was sure of. He just wanted to kill John Fowler, and he really thought he had succeeded. For a few days, he had all but howled at the moon he was so angry when he found out John was really alive.

Bruce and John had a special hate/hate relationship. Bruce hated John, and he hated his father for acting like John was the son he never had. Just because Bruce wasn't the same man that stood up for truth, justice, the American way, apple pie, baseball, and whatever outdated insane idea his father stood for didn't mean Jeremiah Cosby should favor John over him. John so believed in the value of life that it made Bruce physically ill sometimes. What was unusual for Bruce was John wasn't the center of his thoughts right now. No, that spot was held for a member of John's team, the computer freak, Chet.

Chet had put three bullets into Bruce. The fight between Bruce and John had been personal. So Bruce had shot John in front of his little group of merry men, or would that be merry people? Bruce shook his head, frustrated. Political correctness made him sick. It made him want to kill someone. Bruce smiled; thinking about killing always made him smile. He looked back down at the book he was studying. It was about the nerves in the back and what could cause paralization. The footsteps outside stopped at his door; it was the attendant. Bruce put the book down as the attendant opened the door, and someone came inside. Bruce smiled to see his lawyer, Arnold.

"Hello, Arnold," Bruce said, never rising from his seat. Arnold nodded to his client. He waited for the attendant to shut the door and his footsteps to fade down the hall before he spoke.

"I've come to warn you," Arnold began. "There is word that someone might want to free you from your confinements in exchange for a favor. If that happens, then you must never go with them of your own free will." The entire time Arnold was speaking, he was nodding and smiling. Bruce understood that Arnold was trying to send him a coded message. Bruce enjoyed a bit of silliness as much as the next person. Well, okay, he didn't, but it made the attendants in the ward nervous, and that was fun. Bruce returned the smile and decided to play along with the charade.

"Thank you, Arnold," Bruce replied. "Do you have any idea what they would want me to do, not that I would ever entertain such a horrible notion?"

"I think they would want you to continue with your plan," Arnold said, nodding down to the book in Bruce's lap. Bruce smiled even broader. Paralyzing Chet almost made Bruce smile as much as the thought of killing someone, if not more so.

"I will be vigilant in watching for these scoundrels and will fight them off with my every breath," Bruce said, shaking his head the entire time. He stopped and thought for a second. It was time for him to throw the first monkey wrench in the plans of those who now thought they controlled him. "Please let them know the message is received loud and clear." Arnold nodded. "One more thing," Bruce added, almost as an afterthought. Arnold waited. "I'd like a word with the President of the Senate."

Arnold had to think for a second. After he figured out who that was, he looked very surprised. "I know. It surprised me as well that I want to talk to him, but I need to. We need to understand each other." Arnold waited to make sure that was all Bruce had to say. When he was sure Bruce was done, he yelled for the attendant. He left Bruce who was back to studying. Outside, he looked back at the hospital.

"Oh, Bruce," Arnold said quietly to himself. "What you forget is who pays my bill and who I report to." Arnold paused, shook his head, and continued. "I am so going to miss you and your insanity."

**Archibald Staples, Minimum Security Prison
Now**

Chapter 23

Archibald did something he never did. He went to church. Well, not church exactly, he went to the prison ministry meeting. Archibald didn't believe in God. Archibald believed in Archibald. Archibald had always taken care of himself and didn't believe in any power other than that of one's self. Today's sermon was being given by a visiting preacher, Adam Johnson. Archibald took a seat and half listened to the sermon. The preacher was talking about how the road to forgiveness begins by admitting one's sins. Archibald thought about all of things that he had done over his life. Tears started to form in his eyes.

One of the trustees of the prison, and a consistent member of the congregation, saw Archibald. Archibald began to weep more and more. The trustee couldn't believe what he was seeing. One of the biggest crooks and supposed criminals of all times was weeping in church. As the invitation was given, Archibald seemed to want to do something but wouldn't move. He looked around and made eye contact with the trustee. The look of heartbreak on Archibald's face made the trustee walk over to Archibald.

"Do you want to go down and talk to the preacher?" the trustee asked. Archibald shook his head, sobbing.

"I've done so much wrong," Archibald said, still sobbing. A guard had watched everything going on and stepped toward the back of the church. He radioed in for the warden.

"What's wrong?" the warden asked. The warden's biggest concern with Archibald was the possibility of Archibald taking over the prison.

"You aren't going to believe this," the guard began. "I think Archibald is about to get religion."

"What!?" the warden's voice blasted over the radio.

"He's sobbing and talking about all the things he's done wrong," the guard responded. "Warden, do you know what would happen if Archibald Staples spilled his guts in here? Do you know what that could do for your career?"

The warden began to think. If Archibald confessed to all of his crimes, who knew how many unsolved, and not even opened, cases would be solved? The political windfall would be enormous. A run at a senate or a representative seat would be possible with that kind of media exposure.

"What do we need to do?" the warden asked, seeing his future blossom in his head.

"Let me find out," the guard replied and turned off the radio. He walked over to Archibald and the trustee.

"Archibald," the guard began. "Do you need to talk to the preacher?" Archibald nodded, still sobbing. "Do you want me to take you to him?" Archibald shook his head.

"Private," Archibald got out through tears.

"It could be a few days," the guard answered. Archibald nodded.

"Thank you," he managed. He took the guard's hand while his other hand covered his face while he sobbed. "I've done so much, so much wrong. Thank you for helping me." The guard was stunned. He awkwardly put his hand on Archibald's shoulder.

"I'll get a meeting set up," the guard said. "Do you think one will be enough?" Archibald removed the hand from his face and looked up at the guard; his eyes sad and lost. Archibald couldn't answer and burst into tears again.

"I'll set up several," the guard answered. Archibald nodded and continued to cry while the congregation sang around him.

John's and Jessica's Apartment
Now

Chapter 24

John stood by the window, looking down at the street. He saw nothing, which was good, and bad. He couldn't shake the feeling that someone had been watching him the past few days every time he left the apartment.

Jessica watched John from her seat at the table. She was working on a case, and as many times as John had asked to help, she continued to refuse. She knew he couldn't hurt himself in helping, but she had to stick to her guns. For the first time since John had returned to the FBI, that feeling of dread started to creep into the back of her head.

She was serious in what she told him. They had to solve this mystery, whatever it was. The person John was seeing wasn't Sam. It was one thing when they were both seeing Sam, but now that this other person was showing up, well, at least Jessica knew it wasn't Sam. John wasn't so sure. When John pressed her to explain why it wasn't Sam, Jessica's answer had been simple; Sam wouldn't do that to them. She wouldn't; that was one thing Jessica knew.

Jessica pushed the thoughts from her mind. She glanced at John and then at the computer. There! She had caught John glancing at the computer. She knew what was going on now. While John was trying to solve the mystery, she knew what he was really doing; avoiding one of her biggest embarrassments ever at the Bureau. She got up from the table, pushing her chair back to make as much noise as possible. John started to turn his head toward her and stopped. Jessica couldn't help but smile. He was trying desperately to protect her.

"I'm a big girl and can own up to my mistakes," Jessica said as she headed toward John. John continued to stare straight ahead. Jessica grinned, came up behind John, and wrapped her arms around him.

"Are you sure about this?" John asked quietly.

"You tell it how you remember it happening," she replied. "Don't soften it up just because you want to protect me." John turned to look at her.

"Some of that stuff isn't in the official report," John replied.

"It's fiction, John," Jessica replied with a grin on her face. "You are writing a fiction book. You have embellished some details to make it a better read."

"But, I don't embellish," John replied. Jessica tried not to roll her eyes. She blew out an exasperated breath.

"I understand that, but you have to remember there is no one out there like you," Jessica said, taking his hands and looking into his eyes. "Everyone will think it's just a story, and they will treat it as such." John looked a little uncomfortable.

"I don't know," he said. "Why do I have to write this thing?"

"Honestly?" Jessica asked. John nodded. "It's the only thing the vice-president, Trip, and I could come up with that would force you to sit out and heal."

"What if I promise to not," John began, but Jessica laid a finger on his lips.

"Don't," she said. "Don't tell me what I want to hear." John's shoulders slumped, defeated.

"Yeah, you're right," he admitted, a grin beginning to form on his face. He thought for a second, and a quizzical look began to grow on his face. "If you don't want me investigating, then why the insistence about figuring out who this girl is we're seeing?"

"I don't want you to have to investigate anything," Jessica admitted. "But, there is no one else I trust with this." John looked away just briefly and then back at Jessica. He tried to keep the guilty look off his face but failed. Jessica began to look irritated. "Who did you tell?"

"Well, it's not so much that," John began. Jessica's hands were on her hips. The look on her face could only be described as, "Go ahead, and dig the grave a little deeper." John stopped, thought, and blurted it out. "Ron." Jessica looked like she might explode.

Chapter 25

"Ron!?" she exclaimed. "Ron!? Why in the world would you bring him in on this!?"

"Because he has no prior background or knowledge of Sam," John said quietly, bracing for another explosion. It didn't come. Jessica still looked irritated, but she was thinking about what John had said, and it was beginning to seem logical to her.

"Almost like an independent third party," she said, taking her hands off her hips and now crossing her arms in front of her. She began to slightly pace as she thought. John thought he just might get out of this without any more yelling. He about jumped out of his skin when Jessica whirled and pointed a finger at him. "Do you trust him?" she asked. John began to grin, causing Jessica's irritation to return, which in turn only made John grin more. "I swear, how Sam never killed you…" John knew he needed to answer her question.

"I don't know," John admitted. "But, he wants something from me; that I know." Jessica couldn't help it. She didn't want to feed his ego any more, but she couldn't help it. She began to chuckle.

"You've spent, what, a few hours, maybe six or seven tops with the man, and you know that he wants something from you," she said more than asked. "You're incredible, John."

"I know," John replied and realized that was the wrong answer from the look on her face. "I mean thanks." Jessica couldn't help but laugh. She put her arms around John's neck. She was inches away from him.

"Write what happened," she said.

"Yes ma'am," John responded. "Can I wait until tomorrow?" Jessica raised an eyebrow.

"Have you got something in mind for tonight?" she asked seductively.

"Yeah," John answered as he broke away from her and headed to the couch. "There's a baseball game on tonight I want to watch."

"Really?" she said quietly where only she could hear. John turned the TV on.

"Oh, rats," he said with a smile on his face. "It's in rain delay." Jessica couldn't help but smirk.

"Nicely played, sir," she said. "Nicely played." She began to walk back toward the table where her work was. As she walked by John who was standing by the back of the couch still grinning like a fool, she pushed him. John went over the couch, as Jessica smiled like she was proud of herself.

"What did you do that for?" John asked, trying not to laugh. "I'm rehabbing an injury here." Jessica came around the couch quickly. She grabbed his tee shirt, smiling.

"You ever pull that again, and your injury will be the least of your concerns," she said, moving in very close.

"I gotcha, didn't I?" John asked.

"Yeah, you did," Jessica answered very quietly. The playful look on her face told John she wasn't answering the question he was asking. "Write it tomorrow."

"Okay," John replied. "Tomorrow."

FBI New York Headquarters
8 Years ago

Chapter 26

John glanced over at Chet who just shrugged his shoulders. They were in the observation room. The two men arrested were being held in separate holding cells, but currently, their landlady was being interrogated by Jessica. How that happened, John and Chet really weren't sure. Usually when the two worked together, John did all the interrogations since he had the ability to read people. He could tell when someone was lying or even hiding something, but he didn't know what. Since he had never really studied how to better interrogate people, he wasn't the best at it. He usually just dug through the evidence until he found what he needed. Right now, there was a certain need for speed with a bomb being involved.

That was where John felt he lost his argument. Jessica was a trained, experienced, and more importantly, good interagator. Chet had been in John's corner, but the second Jessica gave Chet a dirty look, Chet had caved. When they had time, John was going to give Chet a long talk about standing his ground. John was sure it had something to do with Chet's and Jessica's bad start.

John was watching the interrogation and knew something wasn't quite right. Jessica was hammering away at the landlady and had been for thirty minutes. Jessica was right in that the landlady's story didn't remain consistent. The problem was, as John watched the landlady Louise, John was sure that Louise was telling the truth each time she spoke, which wasn't possible. Something was nagging in John's mind, and he wasn't sure what it was. Louise was visibly getting more and more upset each time Jessica questioned her. John shook his head as he continued to listen.

"So, you don't know them very well?" Jessica asked.

"No, I mean they're my tenants, but that's all I know about them," Louise answered. "Richard would have known them better."

"Who's Richard?" Jessica asked.

"My husband," Louise answered. Jessica looked through her notes and then back at Louise.

"Where is Richard?" Jessica asked.

"I'm not sure," Louise said. Jessica shook her head.

"Let's get back to the two men who rented the apartment," Jessica said.

"I barely know them. They've only been here a short time," Louise replied.

"They've rented the apartment for six months," Jessica said. Louise looked confused.

"Are you sure?" Louise asked. Jessica showed her the rental agreement. Louise looked at it like she had never seen it before. John watched the whole thing, sure they were missing something. Everything she said she believed, but some statements just seemed to contradict each other. An agent opened the door.

"Sir," the agent said to John. John turned to him. "Sir, there is a young man here who says he is Louise's son." John nodded and went with the agent. They walked the halls and came to a man who seemed extremely agitated.

"Where is my mother?" the man demanded. John held his hand up.

"Sir, I'm going to need you to calm down," John said as he extended his hand. He had learned a long time ago that offering a handshake had a calming influence on some people. "I'm Special Agent John Fowler, and you are?"

"Richard," he answered, shaking John's hand. Richard did appear to calm a little. "I'm sorry for the outburst, but I was told that my mother had been taken here with two of her tenants."

"Do you know anything about the two tenants?" John asked.

"Mr. Fowler, with all due respect, I need to check on my mother," Richard said. "She's not well."

"What do you mean?" John asked, already fearing the answer.

"She's suffering from Alzheimer's," Richard replied. "And, she has a heart condition. If she gets too upset . . ." Richard trailed off. John was horrified.

"Richard," John began as calmly as possible, even though his insides were in turmoil. "What would happen if your mother got upset?"

"She could possibly have a massive cardiac event," Richard replied. John looked sick at his stomach. Richard took that as confusion. "In layman's terms, she could die."

Chapter 27

John leapt to a nearby desk and picked up the phone, calling the observation room.

"Chet," John barked. "Get Jessica to stop the interrogation right now!" Chet began to beat on the window, and Jessica ignored him. She was in her own world right now. She could see the sweat popping on the brow of her suspect. Louise looked extremely uncomfortable, and she kept clutching at her shoulder. Jessica was breaking her; she could feel it.

"Boss," Chet said into the phone. "She's ignoring me."

"How does the suspect look?" John asked.

"She's breaking, Boss," Chet replied. "She's sweating, fidgeting, and looks very uncomfortable." Chet was proud of Jessica. He was surprised when he thought he heard John swear under his breath.

"She's killing her!" John shouted into the phone. "Get in there, and stop it!" Chet looked at the phone and then bolted out the door down to the interagation room. Chet grabbed the door, but it was locked, and he thought Jessica had the key. Chet rushed back to the phone.

"Boss, she's got the door locked!" Chet exclaimed.

"Shoot the lock off!" John screamed. Chet gulped.

"My gun is in my locker," Chet admitted. John nearly collapsed onto the desk. His elbows were planted on the table with his head down between them, holding the receiver in one hand. As he picked his head up, he noticed something on the wall. He knew he could never get back to the room in time with Jessica going full throttle on the witness, but if he could buy a little time. . . he put the phone up to his mouth.

"Whatever you hear, don't leave the building until you have that woman away from Jessica," John said, seeing his future in the FBI going down the toilet.

"What?" Chet asked.

"Just do it!" John said as he raced across the room to the fire alarm. There was going to be some serious consequences to pay for this one.

FBI New York Headquarters
Jessica Hammerstein

Chapter 28

Jessica couldn't believe the gall of John and his buddy Chet. She nearly had Louise broken and telling the truth, and all those two yahoos kept doing was trying to interrupt her. They were bigger glory hounds than she had ever dreamed possible. Jessica ignored the pounding on the glass behind her, and was very glad she had locked the door and taken the key with her. In just a few minutes, if not seconds, she was going to have what she needed from Louise.

"Louise," she said, smacking the table in front of her making Louise jump. "Concentrate, Louise. You keep telling me slightly different stories. I want the truth, Louise. You know who these men are, don't you?"

"No," Louise replied, gripping her shoulder while she continued to sweat. She appeared very uncomfortable.

"You housed them knowing that they were building that bomb," Jessica pressed on, ignoring Louise's answers.

"No," Louise replied, even weaker and looking more pale.

"You knew what they were!" Jessica shouted over Louise's weak protest.

"I don't know them," Louise answered, nearly sobbing. Jessica's face turned to complete fury. She came out of her seat quickly, throwing the chair backwards against the wall. She was about to unload on Louise when the lights in the room began to flash and an alarm began to scream. Jessica stopped in disbelief and looked around. She couldn't believe the gall of those two. She looked down at Louise and wanted to shake her in frustration.

Louise was putting on quite an act. Her breathing was shallow, and she looked extremely pale. John and Chet were going to pay, but first, she was getting the truth out of Louise if it killed her.

Chapter 29

Richard watched John race across the room, not sure what was going on. As John neared the fire alarm, it dawned on Richard what he was about to do. Terror welled up in Richard as he worried if his mother was okay.

As John approached the fire alarm, he got his feet tangled with each other and began to fall. He reached out and grabbed the handle of the fire alarm as he fell, pulling the little white lever. The alarm began to sound as he crashed to the ground, disorienting himself for a second. His mother had always told him he wasn't the most graceful creature in the world, and he was pretty sure he had just proved her right. He picked himself up and began to head down the hall to the interrogation room as fast as he could. People were filing past him, trying to get out of the building. John thought for a second that this must be how salmon swimming upstream must feel.

As he approached the interrogation room, he noticed nothing had changed. Chet was looking at the door, panicking.

"Get back," John said drawing his gun. "Get the paramedics up here, ASAP!" Chet ran back to the observation room to make a phone call. John walked up to the door and peered into the window. Neither person was near the door, but Louise did not look good. John backed away, muttering under his breath, took aim at the door, and fired twice at the handle. The handle came flying off, and John kicked the door in. The look on Jessica's face was one part complete shock and the other part complete hatred. He ignored Jessica and went to Louise. He put his fingers to her neck and her heartbeat was rapid and weak. Her pulse was threadlike.

"Hold on, Louise," John said. He noticed out of the corner of his eyes that Jessica was starting toward them. He whirled toward Jessica.

"Stay back," he hissed through his teeth. Jessica jumped back in surprise mixed with a little bit of fear. Richard appeared in the doorway.

"Oh, no," Richard moaned. He started digging through his pockets and pulled out a vial. John motioned Richard over to his mother. Jessica started to say something, but John cut her off by grabbing her by the arm and dragging her down the hall to the observation room. He opened the door, scaring Chet, threw her in, followed behind her, and slammed the door shut. She spun around to face him and slapped his jaw.

"You have some nerve, you jerk!" she screamed. Chet was thankful the room was soundproof. "You two want all the glory! Well you've got another thing coming! I'm demanding an investigation be opened into you two! You have no right to treat me like this! I had her on the ropes! She was about to tell me everything!"

"Shut! Up!" John said quietly but fiercely. He grabbed her arm again and dragged her to the window and pointed to Louise. "You nearly killed her!"

Jessica looked at Louise, then over to Chet who sadly nodded his head, back to Louise and then back to John. John's face was covered with rage. It was only then that it dawned on Jessica what she had done.

"Oh, no," she said, tears beginning to run down her face at the horror of what she had done.

Chapter 30

The paramedics arrived shortly and attended to Louise. John left Jessica in the observation room with Chet. John gave specific orders for her to not come out of the room for anything short of a fire, and even then, it was up to Chet's discretion. John found Richard who seemed very relieved.

"It seems she didn't have a myocardial infarction," Richard said. John looked blankly at Richard . "Sorry, she didn't have a heart attack."

"Oh, well, that's good," John said nodding, wondering why people today just couldn't say heart attack.

"It appears it was mostly a panic attack. They think she'll be alright," Richard replied.

"Look, I want to apologize to you for what happened," John said. "The two men had a bomb. Then, your mother gave very inconsistent answers." John paused and ran his hand through his hair. "I'm sorry. We were trying to save lives, not take your mother's." Richard nodded.

"I'm sure she became very confused," Richard said. "I'm the one who set up their contract. Mom just signed off on the contract because everything is still in her name. I need to get her to sign some things over to me for her protection." John nodded.

"Did you know anything at all about them?" John asked. Richard shook his head.

"They seemed like two good old country boys to me," Richard said, shrugging. John nodded.

"One last thing," John began. "She said Richard was her husband."

"He was," Richard replied. "I'm a junior. She sometimes gets us confused." The look on John's face was a mixture of understanding and sorrow for what Richard must be dealing with.

"Look, go be with your mom," John said, gesturing down to the paramedics who were getting ready to wheel Louise--who John thought looked 3000 percent better--out of the building. "If we have any more questions, we'll come talk to you, I promise." John held his hand out, and Richard shook it and headed off to be with his mother. John blew air out of his cheeks.

"Well, that's one mess fixed," John said to himself.

"That's good," came a voice behind him. John closed his eyes and internally groaned. He turned to face Trip. Trip had a look on his face similar to the one John's dad used to have when they would have what was known as "a come to Jesus meeting."

"Trip," John began. Trip smiled and held up a hand.

"Save it, John," Trip replied. "I want to hear this from all three of you at once. I have a feeling your little trio is done before you even got started. Get everyone to my office now." Trip walked past John, chuckling to himself. John wondered if his day could get any worse.

Chapter 31

John walked into the interrogation room. He waved for the other two to join him, so he could tell Chet and Jessica the good news. Jessica entered first, still looking a little upset for what she did. If this wasn't going to get all of them in trouble, John thought he might enjoy this.

"Trip wants us in his office for a meeting," John said quietly to the other two. Chet looked as though he might faint. Jessica set her jaw and nodded.

"I guess this little trio is over before it even starts," Jessica said, determined to take her share of the blame. John blew out a breath and ran his hand through his hair. He knew that he wanted Jessica to tell everything that she had done, but if she did that, then the trio probably was over, and that wasn't what Sam wanted.

"Would you agree that Chet and I owe you one?" John asked Jessica cautiously. Jessica looked amused.

"At least," she responded with a slight smile.

"I might, emphasize, might, know a way out of this mess, but it will require you to let me take the lead," John said, hoping she would demand to fall on her sword. Jessica gave him a level look.

"Would you be lying in what you say?" Jessica asked. Chet snorted.

"You know it makes him nearly break out in hives to lie, right?" Chet asked. "I mean he could lie to criminals or in a situation like that, but when it comes to friends, coworkers, or his boss, it's nearly impossible for him to lie." Chet paused and thought for a second. "Although, he does sometimes tell certain versions of the truth." Jessica looked at Chet and then back at John. She raised an eyebrow.

"Certain versions of the truth?" she asked. John grinned.

"Say you're late for work, and you walk in and say, "Hey, my aunt's in the hospital." Most people will let it go at that as to why you were late," John said. Jessica was slowly nodding.

"He never said he was late because of that," Chet replied with a grin. Jessica looked at Chet and then back to John. John's grin was turning into more of a smirk.

"Oh, good grief," Jessica moaned, covering her head with her hands. She raised her head up. "If you get caught -"

"You're screwed regardless," John said, still smirking. Jessica closed her eyes.

"You two are terrible, you know that?" Jessica asked.

"Hey, we didn't almost give Louise a myocardial infarction," John said. Jessica looked at John, confused. "A heart attack." Jessica turned pale and looked like she might throw up. John now understood why people didn't say heart attack. It was much more powerful to have to explain the term. John filed that away for future use.

"You can't spell myocardial infarction," Chet said to John. John thought for a second and had to nod in agreement.

"I may be sick," Jessica said. They both turned to Jessica.

"We should probably hurry to Trip's office then," Chet said. John nodded.

"Do you think he would take pity on me if he tried to fire me, and I got sick on his desk or carpet?" Jessica asked.

"Nope," John answered. "But, it would really upset him, and that I would love to see." Jessica groaned again as John opened the door and ushered them down the hall to Trip's office.

Chapter 32

"Would you like to explain what happened?" Trip asked, looking amused. John looked at Chet who shook his head. John looked at Jessica. She looked a little uncertain and then following Chet's lead, shook her head. John looked back at Trip. John pushed his upper lip between his lower gum and lower lip and shook his head slightly but quickly.

"Nope," John answered. The amusement left Trip's face. John began to grin. "You did ask, sir." Trip began to look a bit angry. John loved getting Trip off his game. Trip was so by the book, and John couldn't locate the book on many things. He didn't break the big rules, but the little ones--he felt--were all up to interpretation. He knew in his mind since lying bothered him, that breaking the rules wasn't consistent. The way John saw it, the rule book was created by someone else, and when John spoke, it was his words. John had his own rules he would never break, but someone else's rules, well, that was up to interpretation. That was how he worked it out in his mind. John believed you didn't kill, and you didn't steal. Beyond that, everything else was negotiable.

"What happened?" Trip demanded.

"Well, we were at a party," John began.

"I know that," Trip growled. John looked confused.

"Then, sir, I'm confused. What did you want to know?" John asked.

"The fire alarm," Trip somewhat growled.

"It went off," John answered. Trip was glaring at John and not looking at the other two, which was probably best. Jessica looked like she was about to faint, or throw up, or both.

"How!?" he barked.

"I pulled it," John replied nonchalantly. Trip didn't see that answer coming. His eyes got caught in his head, and he started to stutter.

"W-ww-wh-what?" he finally blurted out.

"I tripped, and as I fell, I put my hand out to catch something," John explained calmly as if he was explaining how to make toast.

"I don't understand," Trip began.

"Well, sir, it seems I'm not too graceful, and I sometimes trip over my own feet," John began. "I think we might want to bring up to the safety committee that they need to put a cover over the alarm."

"They do that in some schools," Chet said. John turned to Chet as Trip looked on, stunned.

"I've seen that," John said. "It's so the kids won't pull them as a game. It ends up costing the schools lots of money for those false alarms." Chet nodded and turned toward Trip. John followed his lead and did the same. Jessica stood back watching, starting to believe she might get out of this jam.

"You know, sir, you should probably be the one to bring this up to someone about safety," Chet said. "It would surely save money in the long run than someone pulling a fire alarm accidently." Trip nodded absently. All he could wonder was what was going on.

Chapter 33

"You know there are some companies that recognize employees for money saving ideas," Chet said to John. John nodded.

"I wonder if the FBI does that?" John asked. Chet shrugged.

"I don't know, but if they don't, you and I should suggest that, and we can use Trip's idea for the security covers as the first one," John replied. John turned toward Trip. "You would be okay with that, right, sir?" John asked Trip. Trip wasn't sure what to say.

"I mean, it would be nice to receive an award, but it really isn't my idea," Trip said, wondering how they had gotten here.

"I'm pretty sure it was, sir," John said. Chet nodded, and they both turned toward Jessica. She looked at John and Chet and slowly nodded. John clapped his hands together. "There! It's settled."

"Are you okay, agent?" Trip said to Jessica, finally noticing her and how pale she was. He was going to get things back on track and end this travesty here and now. John smiled.

"Trip, she was great!" John exclaimed. The growing smile fell from Trip's face as he looked at John. The only way to describe the look on Trip's face was incredulous. Chet covered the smile growing on his mouth with his right hand while holding his right elbow with his left hand. He just prayed no one looked too closely at his eyes as they might give him away.

"I was?" Jessica asked, utterly confused.

"Trip, someday, we should really have Jessica teach on how to spot inconsistencies within an interview," John said, smiling at Jessica. "I have to admit that she is amazing at it." Trip was even more stunned than before.

"What about the paramedics?" Trip asked. At this point, he had all but given up hope of breaking them up. John nodded slowly with a sad look on his face.

"It was almost unfortunate collateral damage," John said, still looking sad. "We had to make a call, and these men had a bomb. We had to find out information quickly and weren't able to do proper vetting of the subject we questioned." John stopped for a second and frowned. "Subject seems so impersonal, don't you think?" he asked Trip. Trip couldn't help but nod. Where did he lose control, he wondered.

"Her name was Louise," John continued. "She suffered from Alzheimer's, and we were unaware. As soon as we were, we did everything in our power to put her first." John shook his head again, leaned forward and put his hands on the back of the chair in front of him. "It's not a pretty world we live in anymore, sir. We had to worry about the possibility of another bomb, and it almost cost Louise her life. Now, I know what you're thinking."

"You do?" Trip asked, having no idea what he was thinking or where this was going.

"How can we prevent this from happening?" John asked, barreling on through. "Sir, that is an excellent question, one I'm afraid I don't have the answer to. I would like to submit to your judgment on that, and when you have protocol on how to handle any future similar situations, I suggest we have an agency wide SOP put in place." Trip nodded slowly. His head really hurt. He felt like he had been run over by a truck.

"What about the two men who built the bomb?" Trip asked, fearing any answer.

"We have yet to question them," John answered.

"They were extremely drunk," Chet added. "They weren't very coherent."

"We know that expediency is warranted since bombs were involved, but we're very tired, sir," John said. "Do you mind if we get some sleep and get back to this in the morning?" Trip looked relieved.

"Go," Trip said. "Go, and when you get back in the morning, I want you to find out answers from those two." John thought about saluting, but thought that would be going too far. They filed out of Trip's office with John bringing up the rear. John couldn't resist.

"Sir," John said. Trip looked up. Defeat was clear on his face. "You have a good night," John said with his famous smirk on his face. He shut the door quickly before Trip could respond. Trip waited until he couldn't hear the footsteps any longer and pulled out his cell phone. He punched in some numbers and waited for the voice on the other end.

"Jeremiah," Trip said. "You were right. Tonight was their first test, and they stood up for each other. I think we've found what you were looking for." Trip nodded to what Jeremiah was saying. "I agree, sir. I'll call back with any more progress. Good night." Trip disconnected the call and rubbed his temple.

"Submit to my judgment?" Trip muttered out loud. "What kind of idiot does he take me for?" Trip began to chuckle to himself.

Chapter 34

Laughter rolled through Trip's office. John had just finished reading the newest section of the manuscript to Trip, Chet, Jessica, and Ron. Trip was nearly crying he was laughing so hard, Ron was belly laughing, Chet looked as though he might pass out he was laughing so hard, and Jessica managed to look slightly ashamed while laughing.

"This is how you three started?" Ron asked. John nodded, surprised his friends had enjoyed the story as much as they did. "How long did you know that Trip knew?"

"I had a little talk with John a few days ago," Trip replied, wiping the tears from his face. "I asked him to keep everything I was telling him under wraps until I could see the reactions on their faces. Was it ever worth it!" Jessica continued to laugh but still looked slightly embarrassed.

"Does anyone know what happened to Louise?" Jessica asked. John smiled and nodded.

"She's living with her son," John replied. "She's doing pretty well. Richard says she has some bad days but mostly good days." Jessica smiled and nodded. "He did ask that you never come visit her," John added. Trip roared with laughter again, and Chet and Ron joined him. John was fighting the smile on his face, while Jessica was trying not to laugh while appearing irritated at the same time.

"John, you have to get this published," Ron said. John just shook his head.

"I thought better of you than that, Ron," John replied.

"Ignore him," Jessica told Ron. "He doesn't believe anyone when you tell him how good the story is." Ron shrugged.

"I imagine you could write a whole collection of novels," Ron said. John groaned and got up to leave.

"Hold up a second, John," Trip said. "I need to talk to you." Trip looked around the room. It was a friendly look, but they knew it meant to get out.

"Bye, sweetie," Jessica said, coming over to John and wrapping her arms around his neck. John couldn't help but begin laughing. They both turned as one to look at Trip. Trip looked slightly annoyed.

"GET!" Trip barked. Jessica gave John a peck on the lips and left, shutting the door behind her. "Everything okay at home?" Trip asked. John looked confused.

"Yeah," John replied. "Why would you ask me that?" Trip nodded a second and gestured for John to sit down.

"Ron has come to me," Trip began. John rolled his neck to release the tension. He wasn't happy. Trip held up his hand to hold back John's explosion so he could explain. "I think you made the right call." John's eyes widened in surprise. "It's probably best to leave the rest of us out of it, but if you find you need help, we're here." John pressed his lips together, thinking.

"This is about other stuff, isn't it?" John asked. Trip grinned as he nodded.

"I'd like to think of us as more of a family now, John," Trip replied. "Whoever this girl is, Chet and I are here to help. We only run this up the chain if there is no other choice, okay?" John nodded, stood, and headed to the door. He turned back to Trip.

"Sam had you in on it from the beginning, didn't she?" John asked. Trip shrugged, but a grin covered his face. "I'm sorry, Trip," John said. It was Trip's turn to

91

look surprised. "I should have given you a chance back then. You had nothing but our best interests at heart. I'm sorry." John then turned and left. Trip sat back at his desk, put his feet up, and smiled.

"No apology necessary," Trip said to the empty room.

Chapter 35

John hadn't been in the building since the shooting and decided to take a look around. Where Bruce's huge office used to be was gone. Once again, the wall was gone, and cubicles filled the area. Several agents recognized him and came over and talked to him. John usually hated these types of meetings with people, but for some reason this time, it didn't seem to bother him. After a little while, he made his way down to the foxhole. Jessica was leaning against what John had come to think of his working desk. It was just an old desk but very large. John loved to open up all the things he thought related to a case and put them on the desk, so he could easily scan from one thing to the next. Jessica had a smirk on her face.

"Told you he'd come down here," Jessica said. Ron was at what appeared to be his new desk, but Chet was nowhere to be seen. John looked at all the monitors and computers.

"Is it my imagination, or does he have more?" John asked, referring to the electronics. Jessica nodded, almost exasperated.

"He's convinced Trip he needs more to track down any relationship between Archibald and the rest of his group, whoever they are," Jessica replied. John nodded. John didn't keep secrets from Jessica now that they were married, except for one. It wasn't really a secret since Jessica didn't believe him anyway. John was convinced that former President Nichols was in with Duck and Archibald. The problem was there was no proof, and John couldn't convince his two friends yet. John looked around.

"Seems mostly the same," John offered. Jessica nodded, still smirking. Chet appeared from behind the setup of computers.

"Why are you here?" Chet asked, looking perturbed.

"Lost a bet?" John asked. Chet nodded. John frowned. Jessica laughed and went over to her locker. She pulled out a DVD, came back, and handed it to Chet. "That's the bet?" John asked. Chet nodded, and John relaxed. Chet had gotten into real trouble with gambling in the past. In the end, it had helped lead to the connection between Duck and Archibald, but John never wanted to see his friend go through that again.

"I have to watch Jessica's choice of MMA fights since I lost," Chet replied. Ron suddenly seemed interested and came over. Chet handed him the DVD, and Ron scanned it over.

"Is this the one where he," Ron began.

"Tried to throw a spinning back fist and missed?" Jessica asked, looking perturbed. "Yeah, it is." Ron smiled at Jessica.

"Big fan?" he asked. Jessica smiled and nodded.

"I've watched it for years. Feel free to watch it," Jessica said. "This one here is a little squeamish," she said, jerking her thumb toward John. "I try not to watch the DVDs at home, only the live events." She turned toward John. "Now, back to Chet's question, why are you here?"

Chapter 36

"I've been thinking, and I think Chet will back me up on this," John began. Chet moaned, and Jessica smiled.

"Just write the blasted book," Chet almost moaned. "We know what happened. It will be fine."

"She could lose her career," John said, turning toward his friend. Jessica was amused.

"I could have lost my career," Chet retorted.

"No, you couldn't have. They would have just given you one of those talks," John responded.

"Do they realize you're standing right here?" Ron asked Jessica quietly so as not to interrupt the back and forth.

"They do this often," Jessica replied, still amused. "But, you're right." She turned back to John and Chet and raised her voice. "I am right here you know, and neither one of you have to fight my battles," she said, giving both of them looks. Chet looked somewhat ashamed, but John, well, John looked a little defiant.

"I know you can fight your own battles," John replied. "What I also know is this could get you in all sorts of trouble."

"It's a book!" Jessica exclaimed.

"Do you have the okay to write this?" Ron asked. John turned to look at Ron and then slowly looked at Jessica.

"I don't know, do I?" John asked. Jessica smiled.

"Yes, you do," she responded. "It's fiction." John started to respond, but she put a finger over his mouth. "It's fiction, and that's the end of the story." John sighed and gave up for now. John reluctantly nodded. Jessica smiled and lowered her finger from his mouth. "Now, you can look around for a bit, but then, you're going home. You are not allowed to be here until you finish the projects I gave you." John sighed, nodded, and looked over at Chet.

"Why did you bet I wouldn't be here?" John asked. Chet smiled and shrugged.

"I thought you would, Boss," Chet replied. "But, I've got your back regardless." John smiled at his friend and turned toward Jessica.

"Hear that?" he asked. "He's got my back."

"I heard," she replied, shaking her head at the two of them. "Now go. Finish the book." She took a sideways look at Ron. "Finish your other assignment." Ron looked right back at her. Jessica shook her head and turned back to her husband. "And, then, get back here. We need you, John," she added quietly. John nodded, said his good-byes, and left. Part of him wondered if he didn't solve his current case, if this could be the last time he left the foxhole.

FBI New York Headquarters
8 Years ago

Chapter 37

Jessica rubbed her temple with her hands. Jessica had been interviewing the two prisoners going on eight hours. This was taking longer than she thought. While Jessica was picking up inconsistencies from the two men, it didn't matter. They weren't afraid of anything. There was no threatening them. When Jessica had mentioned the possibility of sending one of the men to Guantanamo, his face lit up like a Christmas tree. That was Bubba Ray; his name had been changed legally. He had basically told Jessica he would love to go there and have the chance to kill some of the other prisoners that were nonbelievers. Well, that's what he said plus a whole lot of racial slurs to every race on the earth. The other prisoner, Eugene, just didn't care. Jessica knew she could find out what she needed. The problem was it was just going to take forever, and she wasn't sure how long they had.

A cup of coffee was placed in front of her. She glanced up and saw John. She smiled gratefully at him. John had given her free reign on the interrogation. She was surprised given what had happened yesterday, but he had been nothing but supportive so far.

"You're on the right track," he said encouragingly. Jessica nodded. "You'll crack them." Jessica looked back up at John, not sure how to begin. John must have read her face because he sat down at the table with a concern look on his face. "Jessica, you're going to get them to crack." Jessica shook her head.

"It's not that I can't crack them," Jessica began. "It's that we're up against the clock, and I don't know how much time we have left." She looked John right in the eye; he could see the worry and concern. "If we don't figure this out, and these two idiots get someone killed because I took too long to crack them, I'm never going to forgive myself."

The two hadn't noticed Trip walking by the room. He had stood outside and listened to the conversation. He had stayed back all day watching the team work together. They were doing a great job. He knew that John couldn't know that Trip thought this team was a good idea, or John would never go for it. Trip smiled. The reverse psychology that was going on was starting to make Trip's head hurt, but it was necessary. Trip moved where he could glance at Jessica. She looked worn out. She had done more than he knew was possible to make the two suspects crack, but nothing worked. He knew she was worried about the bomb, but it was obviously time to take a break.

"I hate to interrupt," Trip said as he came in the room.

"Then don't," John muttered under his breath. Jessica had to choke back a chuckle. Trip acted like he didn't hear but shot John a look. Trip placed a file on the table.

"This just came back from the profilers and a few other specialists," Trip said. John picked up the folder and began to leaf through it, confusion covered his face as he looked up at Trip.

"What is this?" John asked.

"Some type of manifesto," Trip replied. John handed Jessica a folder that had the same copies in it. Trip continued. "Maybe you should take a break, go home, and look this stuff over. Or even better, just go home and look this stuff over tomorrow." John nodded absently as he studied the folder. "You're going to work on this all night, aren't you?" John continued to nod absently. Jessica was fighting back a smile, while Trip just continued to stare at John. John continued to pore over the folder, ignoring Trip. "John!" John looked up at Trip and smiled.

"Night," he said as he headed out the room and went home. Trip shook his head, turned toward Jessica, and jerked his head toward the door, telling her to go. As he watched them leave, he hoped the plan to put them together would work. If it didn't, he was afraid he was going to strangle John.

John and Sam's Apartment
That Night

Chapter 38

John sat at dinner just staring at his plate.

"How was your day, honey?" Sam asked. John grunted and nodded. Sam looked at John for a second and then just nodded. She continued to eat as she spoke to him.

"Mine was interesting," Sam replied. John nodded and continued to stare at his plate. Sam slowly nodded her head and continued. "We might be writing a new grant to get funding for some new equipment." John continued to nod. "I was asked to write it, since I wrote the last one that was just approved." John continued to nod, and now, his eyes slid over to the case file that was on the corner of the table at which he normally worked, and then to the board he kept at home that he used to go over cases. Sam smiled and blew air up with her bottom lip. "I may have to write it with Rodrigo," she went on. She picked up her glass and began swirling its contents, her husband still oblivious. "You know, the one that has the sexy accent." John blinked twice and slowly turned back towards his wife.

"I'm sorry," John began.

"You can say that again," Sam said with a smile splitting her face. She took a drink, and John had to smile.

"I've got a case on my mind," he admitted.

"It doesn't take Sherlock to figure that one out," she replied.

"The chase is afoot, Watson," he replied with a smile on his face.

"Is it a three pipe problem?" she asked, grinning.

"At least," John replied with a chuckle.

"So, tell me about it," she replied, getting up and beginning to clear the dishes. She saw the look on his face and knew he wasn't ready to talk yet. She walked over and put her hands over his, stopping him from helping her. He looked up into her eyes. "Then, go work on it," she said softly. John grinned.

"Did anyone ever tell you that you're amazing, and I'm the luckiest guy on the face of the earth?" he asked. Sam cocked her head and looked off in the distance, thinking.

"Not in the last day or so," she replied, looking back at him. John kissed her and then pulled her in tight. She gently pushed him away. "You're going to ignore me through dinner and then expect me to just have big fun with you?" John grinned.

"Uh-huh," he replied, kissing her. She pushed him off.

"Solve it," she said, pointing at the board. "And, maybe we'll talk," she added quietly with a shy smile on her face.

"Done!" he exclaimed. John quickly raised his eyebrows twice, kissed her on the forehead, and bounded across the living room to set up the board. Sam watched him and shook her head. She loved John, but some days it took all she had to remember how his mind worked. She turned her back and began clearing the dishes when all of a sudden she was swept off her feet. She let out a "Whoop!"

"I'm sorry for ignoring you earlier," John said, his lips inches from hers. Sam smiled at him and leaned up to kiss him, not worrying about the dishes.

Chapter 39

"Do you want anything from the fridge?" Sam yelled to John a few hours later.

"Nah," John responded. Sam shrugged. That was a good sign; he was at least acknowledging her questions. Sam grabbed an apple and headed into the living room where John was slowly pacing the floor looking at the board. John had been working on this for a while now and was no closer to solving it than he was at dinner. Sam looked at the manifesto that had been written. Something about it looked very familiar to her.

"Can I ask you about that?" she asked, nodding her head toward the board. John stopped his pacing and nodded.

"Yeah, that might actually help," John replied. He sat down on the couch while Sam sat in the rocking chair.

"Who wrote this?" she asked. John shook his head.

"Some cultist," John replied. Sam crinkled her nose and looked at the manifesto again. Something wasn't right.

"Have you profiled him?" she asked. John looked at her, and made an impressed face, and nodded. Sam smiled back. John dug through some papers and pulled up what had been found.

"This is the quick one. The profilers have a lot more 'credible' threats than this one to work on," he replied. John looked at the sheet and began to read. "Mid-thirties, uneducated - "

"No," Sam said, shaking her head. John looked up from the sheet he was reading with an eyebrow raised. Sam shot back a defiant look and bit into her apple.

"You have a theory?" John asked. Sam looked at the manifesto, then to John and then back at the manifesto. She looked back at him, bit into her apple, and nodded.

"I think - " she began, but John cut her off with a wave of his hand. "What are you doing?" John was on the

102

phone. He turned to her with the phone cradled on his shoulder.

"I'm calling my two new partners," he replied. "I'm supposed to be a team player now, remember?" Sam shot John a look but smiled, knowing she had been defeated. She was the one that pushed for him to get a team, and now that he had one, she had to realize things would change. She wasn't going to be his sounding board on every single thing anymore. She bit into the apple and wondered if his two new comrades would hate her for that.

Chapter 40

A little while later, the doorbell sounded, and Sam answered the door. It was Jessica.

"Hello, Jessica," Sam said warmly. "Come in."

"Is this okay?" Jessica asked. "Us getting together like this? It's getting late, and I know you have to work tomorrow." Sam smiled at Jessica.

"Are you kidding?" Sam asked. "If I let him stew about this all night, I would never get any sleep."

"How do you put up with him?" Jessica asked and then stopped. She realized, with horror, what she had just said, and who she said it to. She expected Sam to say something or at least be offended, but not Sam. Sam laughed and leaned in to her.

"You know, you were assigned to him, but I chose to marry him. What does that say about me?" she asked with a smile on her face.

"That you're truly a saint?" Jessica offered as she entered the apartment. Sam shut the door and put her arm around Jessica.

"I need to apologize to you," Sam said. Jessica looked at her, confused. "I wanted you on this team," Sam admitted. "I've known the senator for some time, and when he approached me with the idea, he asked me if I would help him. I wanted someone that would stand up to John, and I chose you." Sam decided not to tell Jessica about the conversation she and John had the night of the gala. She wasn't sure how Jessica would have taken that conversation. Jessica stopped and turned to face Sam. "I'm sorry if he's made you miserable. If you want off this crazy train, I can take care of him," she said, pointing her thumb over her shoulder at John. "I can also call the senator, and it won't reflect poorly on you, I promise." Jessica shook her head.

"He doesn't deserve you," Jessica said. Sam smiled.

"I know," she replied. Jessica laughed out loud. "I need someone I trust to watch over him."

"You don't know me," Jessica said. Sam smiled and looked over at John who was ignoring Jessica purposely.

"I know him, and what he means in his coded language," Sam said, turning back to Jessica. "He trusts you to watch his back." Jessica looked over at John who was still ignoring her. She stuck her tongue out at his back, and Sam had to put her hand over her mouth to cover her laugh. "He really irritates me too sometimes," Sam admitted quietly. Jessica turned toward Sam and couldn't figure out what such a nice person could see in the arrogant goofball that was her partner.

"I'll watch him for you," Jessica said, squeezing Sam's hand. "It's a shame. I think we could be great friends, but he wouldn't like it." Sam cocked her head to the side slightly and smiled.

"And, why would Captain Dodo over there have to know?" Sam replied. Jessica smiled at Sam, and the two turned to join John and Chet.

John and Jessica's Apartment
Now

Chapter 41

Jessica looked up from what she had been reading on the laptop with a look of surprise on her face. John had his trademark smirk on his face.

"You knew about that?" Jessica asked, surprised.

"Sam had told me about your little exchange. As far as you two being chummy later on, no, I wasn't aware of that. Of course, I wasn't aware of a lot then," John admitted with a far off look on his face. Jessica silently admonished herself for that, but John saw the look on her face and waved his hand away in annoyance. "Oh, quit that. It's not like that. I was just wondering if you and I hadn't been at odds so much or whatever it was that was between us, if you two wouldn't have been closer, sooner." Jessica gave him a warm smile.

"Did you ever think that maybe we didn't let the rest of you three know?" Jessica asked. John wasn't shocked too often, but this was one of those times. He didn't say anything, but he didn't need to. Jessica knew that look. John was playing things back in his mind. It took just a couple of seconds, but a knowing smile covered John's face.

"That makes complete sense," he said. "Well played, Mrs. Hammerstein, well played."

"It's Mrs. Fowler now," she replied with a mock, proper tone. "Do you mean you really didn't know? I just thought you were going along with things." John shook his head as he sat down on the couch beside her.

"You two got me," he said.

"Yes!" Jessica exclaimed as she brought her arm down with a closed fist. John couldn't help but laugh.

"Why hide it?" he asked. Jessica looked at him like he had just asked the stupidest question ever.

"You mean, why tell you and Chet, the original boys club, Trip, the man who made it seem like our teaming up was the worst idea ever, that your wife and I were besties?" Jessica asked. John thought for a second, slowly nodded, started to say something, stopped, and started the cycle again. He looked over at Jessica who had a slow grin crossing her face, just waiting for him to say anything remotely intelligent.

"I've got nothing," John admitted after a bit.

"You can say that again," Jessica mumbled at him. John tried to look hurt as she swung a pillow at him. He reached for the wound on his chest suddenly, and Jessica dropped the pillow to check on him. As soon as it left her hand, she knew she had been tricked. A tickle fight broke out that Jessica knew she couldn't win. Who knew that after the start the two of them had, she would never find herself happier than she was with John right then and there?

John and Sam's Apartment
8 Years Ago

Chapter 42

"I'd like to thank you all for joining me tonight," John began. Jessica looked around the room, confused. "Something wrong, Miss Hammerstein?"

"I was looking for the congregation of people you seem to be talking to," Jessica replied. John wasn't amused. He continued.

"I've called you here tonight," he began.

"If you say to accuse someone of muuurder, I'm out," Jessica said. Sam was crying; she was trying so hard to hold in her laughter. Chet was red faced from trying not to laugh. John still wasn't amused. John just stared at Jessica for a minute or so. Jessica returned the stare, never blinking. John finally just handed the marker over to Sam and sat down. Sam looked confused. John just shook his head and gestured to the big board.

"Well, I'm not sure what to do," Sam began. "But, the reason John called was because I disagreed with the profiler about your suspect." Jessica had a bewildered look on her face.

"Not to be rude," Jessica began. John looked over at Chet. Chet shook his head. Sam shot John a look to be quiet and gestured to Jessica to continue. "Like I said, not to be rude, but these profilers are experts. What makes you think they're wrong?" Sam nodded.

"First off, John said this was a quick profile and that there were cases that had more credible threats, so I'm guessing you may have not gotten someone's best work," Sam replied. Jessica nodded, impressed. Sam continued. "Secondly, I think they saw exactly what they were meant to see." John and Chet looked at each other at the same time, intrigued. Jessica pulled out a pen and a piece of paper to take notes. John leaned forward, listening intently. Sam froze.

"Uh, guys. I'm just taking a shot in the dark here. I can't promise I'm right," she said, a little nervous.

"We've gotten nowhere on the other profile. Maybe you'll hit something that will help us find a new lead," John said. Jessica nodded. Chet had his laptop out, ready to use it if need be. Sam shrugged and continued.

"You said that the person who wrote this was mid-thirties and uneducated," Sam said. Everyone nodded. "Both of those, in my opinion, are wrong." John smiled. Sam looked a little nervous but continued. "Look at the words. They aren't the words of someone uneducated, and they are used correctly in all the sentences." Sam pointed to two of the sentences that read, "Our perpis is to forever be a part of the gloreais cindome," and "We are stane by our faith and do not have to abdute others to grow."

"The sentences' structure isn't one of someone who is uneducated," Sam said. She read the sentences aloud, "Our purpose is to forever be a part of the glorious kingdom. We are sustained by our faith and do not abduct others to grow." She looked at the group and continued. "I think the person who said these words may be mid-thirties, but the person, or persons, who is writing this manifesto is a lot younger," Sam said. She looked at the three sets of eyes watching her and hanging on her every word. She continued. "I think the writer, or writers, of this manifesto are children, specifically kindergarten to first grade children."

Chapter 43

The looks on John's, Jessica's, and Chet's faces were not what Sam was hoping for. She honestly wasn't sure what she was looking for. She just knew she was not seeing what she had hoped for. The three looked sick.

"Did I do something wrong?" Sam asked. John shook his head.

"No," John said quietly. "I just think the three of us are all bothered by the thought of using children with bombs." Jessica turned to John.

"Does this mean -" she trailed off, not even able to finish the sentence.

"You've got some very religious people, possibly even extremists, and children involved, and two good old country boys that are doing whatever their leader tells them to," John said. Chet and Jessica looked even sicker. "I mean, if that doesn't scream cult, then I don't know what does." Chet winced at the word cult.

"Can we go with religious community until we have more proof?" Chet asked. Sam looked very confused.

"I don't understand," Sam said. John looked at Jessica for some help. Jessica nodded.

"In our world," Jessica began. "Usually when law enforcement and these types of groups meet up -" Jessica couldn't finish.

"People die?" Sam finished the thought for her. Jessica nodded. "I could be wrong," Sam quickly added. John stood up and walked up to the board to study it. He turned to Sam.

"Why do you think that kids wrote this, specifically kindergarten to first graders?" John asked. Sam nodded and went over to the board.

"My guess is someone was telling the children what to write," Sam began. "Kids would never talk with these types of sentences, but look at the words." Sam pointed to the word perpis. "That word is purpose. The child has the beginning of understanding of spelling and sounding out words. A perfect example is this word." Sam pointed to promis. "Kids this age don't hear the e and know to add it to the word." John nodded at the explanation.

"Chet, Jessica, doesn't it make sense that some jerk is walking around spouting this nonsense off while having kids write what he is saying?" John asked. Chet and Jessica looked at each other and shook their heads no. John nodded, smiling. "But, it would if you have delusions of grandeur." Chet groaned and put his hands over his face.

"Cult," he said into his hands. John nodded.

"What's worse is he doesn't want to be caught," John said. "He made it look, at first glance, like he was an uneducated man. Chances are, he or she is extremely educated. He's probably had some dealing with children as a teacher or has a sibling as a teacher."

"Not necessarily, John," Sam said. "He could simply be a father and noticed it." Sam realized she had just corrected him in front of his team and was a little worried about how John would react. He turned to her with a sad look on his face.

"That's even worse because that means he is observant and probably has a high intellect," John said. Sam sighed. This was looking worse and worse.

"Could it be a woman?" she asked, noting the last time John had said "he" only. John thought for a second, but Jessica was the one who answered.

"Do you see a woman doing this to kids, Sam?" Jessica asked. Sam hadn't thought of that.

"I don't think I could, but that doesn't mean one couldn't," she replied. Jessica nodded. "But, if I had to pick one over the other, yeah, it would be a male." Chet continued to sit with his head in his hands.

"These never end well," he mumbled. John didn't say anything. Chet was right. These things never seemed to end well.

Chapter 44

"So, we have a group that is making bombs and has kids," Chet said. Jessica looked like she wanted to throw up. John was a shade of pale that no one had quite ever seen before, and Sam . . . Sam was furious.

"You have to do something!" she screamed at John. John looked at her, his eyes lost.

"What?" John asked. "I don't even know where they are."

"I can find them," Jessica said. John nodded.

"You can," John replied. "But, can you in time?" Chet shot John a look, and Sam smacked his shoulder.

"John, this is not the time!" she admonished. Jessica stood up and shook her head.

"He's not chastising me," Jessica said, looking at John. John was looking right back at her, slowly nodding. "He's telling the truth. These guys are hard to crack and have nothing to fear from us." Sam started to apologize, but John waved her off.

"Jessica can do it," John said. "We just don't know what kind of clock we're up against." Jessica nodded and walked around the apartment. She stopped at the window and stared out over the city. Sam rose from her spot and went over to Jessica. She hesitated a second and then hugged her shoulders from behind.

"You can do this," Sam said quietly. Jessica turned her head and smiled at Sam.

"Thanks," Jessica replied. "But, I need something to work with." She looked over at John. "Do you have any ideas?" John was surprised but began to think.

"Chet could sing to them," John offered, trying to get his mind to work.

"That would be cruel and unusual punishment," Sam quipped, knowing what John was doing and trying to help. Everyone laughed, and Jessica and Sam came back over to the couch where John was sitting and thinking.

"I need something to just get them to slip," Jessica said, searching her brain for anything. John nodded and stared off into space, thinking.

"They're country boys," John said, still looking straight ahead. Jessica nodded but realized John wasn't talking to her. He was working something out in his head. "They've probably known each other forever." Jessica nodded at that assessment. "Bubba Ray's the leader." Jessica nodded at that. A slow grin covered John's face. He turned to Jessica. "Are you ready to try something a little unconventional?"

"I don't know. I think one near death for my interviewees a week is my limit," Jessica replied with a grin. John couldn't help but laugh at that. John thought Jessica actually turned a little red with embarrassment.

"If this works the way I think it will, no one will get hurt," John replied with a smile. Jessica shrugged.

"What do I have to lose?" Jessica asked. John ran his hand through his hair. If this didn't work . . . he didn't want to think what could happen if there was another bomb, and they didn't get to it first.

"Let's get down to the office," John said.

"Now?" Sam asked. John turned toward her, nodding.

"We don't know how much time we have," John explained. Sam nodded, understanding. "It gets worse," John continued. "If we figure this out, we may have to catch a flight somewhere tonight." Sam didn't like this part of the job, but she understood. She got up and headed toward the bedroom. Jessica looked at John, concerned.

"Is she mad?" Jessica asked.

"Nope," John answered, raising his hands to catch the packed overnight bag that came flying out of the bedroom. "We've done this part before." Chet and Jessica laughed. Their hearts weren't in it though. None of them felt good about what could possibly happen.

Chapter 45

A few hours later, Jessica walked back into the room with Bubba Ray and sat down across from him. He looked her up and down again.

"Why don't you just let me go?" Bubba Ray asked. "You haven't caught me doing anything."

"There was a bomb in your apartment," Jessica said.

"It wasn't mine," Bubba replied.

"Your fingerprints are on it!" she exclaimed.

"Weren't mine. Someone must have planted them," Bubba Ray said, leaning toward her. "I would never hurt anyone," he said. He then leaned back, smiled, and added, "That didn't deserve it." Jessica stared at him for a second. Bubba Ray smiled at her.

"I know you think I'm some backwaters hillbilly," he began. Jessica shook her head.

"No one here has ever called you that," she replied.

"I'm not," he continued over top of her. "I'm not the smartest guy in the world, but I knows me a thing or two." He was looking away, almost staring off into space. "There are some people here who would hurt us, and I'm just trying to make sure everyone realizes that. Isn't that protected by my rights?" Jessica shook her head. This was getting nowhere, fast. The door handle shook, and John entered with the other prisoner, Eugene.

"Oh," John began. "I'm sorry. I didn't realize you had this room."

"That's okay," Jessica said. "I'm not getting anywhere with the suspect here."

"Do you mind?" John asked. "The other rooms are full, and I wanted to verify with Eugene here what Bubba Ray told you about neither of them being the leader of the cult."

"John!" Jessica hissed at John. Eugene looked at Bubba in confusion.

"You said you weren't gonna tell them nuthin'!" Eugene yelled at Bubba.

"I didn't, you idgit!" Bubba yelled back.

"So, I shouldn't ask about the second bomb?" John asked Jessica. Eugene shot Bubba a death look.

"You said to never tell that, no matter what!" Eugene screamed. Bubba groaned. John shut the door behind him and shoved Eugene in the chair beside Bubba. John couldn't help but grin as he leaned against the back wall of the interview room.

"Is that the slip you were looking for?" John asked. Jessica turned toward John and smiled warmly.

"It's a start," she replied. "And, it's a good one."

Chapter 46

"Where's the second bomb?" Jessica asked.
Eugene folded his arms in front of him like a pouting child.
Bubba Ray sat very quietly. He looked up at John.

"It's the middle of the night. I know that there are
other interview rooms open," Bubba Ray said, staring at
John. John shrugged.

"You got me," John admitted. He turned to Jessica.
"Look, I didn't eat. Do you mind if I run get something?"
Jessica nodded. "Do you want anything?" he asked her.
She nodded. John turned toward the other two.

"Shoot, yeah," Bubba Ray said. "Something good,
too! I've about had it with those wimpy meals." John
nodded and left. He came back in about ten minutes. He
gave Bubba Ray and Eugene food from one bag, and he
and Jessica got food from another.

"This is a salad," Bubba said. John nodded as he
opened his container. "You've got fried chicken, mashed
potatoes, and what's that?"

"This is cabbage with hot pepper sauce," John
replied. Bubba's lips were starting to smack together. John
was pleased with himself. He thought of going through the
food kept at the two men's apartment earlier. When it
became obvious that they liked many of the same things he
did, he figured that they didn't care for many of the same
foods he didn't. John continued the conversation. "We're
supposed to feed you healthy. That's why you get the
grilled chicken salad."

"It's not vinegar?" Bubba asked, staring at John's
food. Eugene was openly drooling. John shook his head
no. "It's not often you see hot pepper sauce here." John
leaned forward. Bubba and Eugene did the same.

"It's homemade," he said quietly. Jessica was
taking mental notes. She never would have thought of this
line of attack on the two men. She was mentally filing this

idea to use in the future while trying not to laugh at the two suspects. John leaned back in his chair, picked up a fried chicken leg, and bit down. He made a "mmmm" sound. Bubba looked ready to cry.

"Are you sure I can't have some of the fried chicken?" he nearly whimpered. John looked at Jessica who shook her head no. John looked at Bubba, shrugged, and took another bite. He was about to throw in another sound effect when Eugene spoke up.

"I'll tell you everything I know if you get me some of that chicken!" he exclaimed.

"Shut up!" Bubba yelled.

"You shut up!" Eugene yelled back. Jessica started to stop them, but John laid a hand on her arm and shook his head just slightly. The two men ignored them and carried on. "You're always tellin' me what to do, and now look where it's gotten us!"

"I gotta tell you what to do because I'm the smart one!" Bubba replied, his eyes red. Eugene looked furious and glanced over at John. John shrugged, took a bite of mashed potatoes. That was the straw that broke the camel's back. Eugene cracked.

"They got a bomb in Tennessee!" Eugene shouted. John couldn't believe it. They had found what they were looking for. He was sure they could have found out much more, and they probably would have if Bubba hadn't chose that exact second to punch Eugene in the face, breaking several of his teeth.

Chapter 47

"Does someone want to tell me what happened here?" Trip asked several hours later. They were in an empty hallway in the middle of the night after the fight had broken out between the two suspects.

"Not really," John responded. Trip glared at John until Jessica wasn't for sure if Trip was going to punch John.

"It's my fault, sir," Jessica said, stepping in front of John. John rolled his eyes, and using his right arm, he tried to push her from the side so he could talk to Trip. Trip saw John try to physically move her, caught the look on Jessica's face, smiled, and nodded. Jessica mouthed, "thank you," and grabbed John's right arm twisting it behind him and slammed him into the wall, his arm torqued to the point it was about to snap.

"OWWW!" John screamed. His face was red from pain, and his eyes looked like they were about to bug out of his head. Jessica cranked his arm just a little to show him how serious she was, and John yelled louder. Jessica leaned in close to his ear and spoke very softly.

"You don't, EVER get to push me. Do we understand each other?" Jessica asked just above a whisper.

"You stepped in front of me," John countered. Jessica gave the arm another little twist. John really thought his arm was going to break. "Okay! Okay! I won't ever touch you again!" She held him for just a second longer and then whispered where no one else could hear them.

"I didn't say all that. Just don't push me again," Jessica said and let John go. John leapt away from her, wondering if she had gone nuts. What did she mean? John was rubbing his shoulder and arm, trying to not cry in front of his boss and friend. He glared at Jessica. She just looked at him like nothing had happened.

"This is nuts, Trip!" he yelled. "She about took my arm off, and you did nothing about it!" Trip set his jaw and glared back at John.

"You had two of my prisoners trying to reenact wrestling moves in my interrogation rooms!" Trip yelled back. "I'm going to have to let those two go!"

"One of them already agreed to lead us to their leader," John spat back. Trip backed up.

"What?" he asked, clearly surprised.

"We have a signed agreement with one of the prisoners. He's going to take us to the cult's base," John replied. Trip looked over at Chet who nodded. He looked over at Jessica who nodded reluctantly.

"Fine," Trip said. "The three of you take the prisoner, and find this cult. Find the bomb, and shut it down!" Trip spun and headed down the hall. He stopped and headed back. "And, quit beating each other up!" he yelled, spun again, and headed back down the hall. After he turned the corner, Jessica ran up to John to look at his arm.

"Did it pop or come out of place?" she asked, concerned.

"I don't think so," John replied. "Did you have to crank my arm quite so much?"

"You told me to make it look as real as possible," Jessica replied. John looked up at her and smiled.

"I did, didn't I?" John asked, grinning like the village idiot. Jessica shook her head, surprised the plan had worked.

Chapter 48

Blood was flowing out of Eugene's mouth.

"What'd you hit me for!?" Eugene yelled at his brother.

"Because you're being stupid!" Bubba yelled back. Jessica had regained her composure first. If either man had attacked either agent, John or Jessica would have been ready, but for Bubba to attack Eugene, it just took both of them by complete surprise. John ran to the door and yanked it open. Chet was waiting in the hallway after John had gone to get the food.

"Bubba attacked Eugene!" John yelled at Chet. Chet groaned, got on his cell phone, and started making a phone call. John started to go back in when he looked down at the observation room door. He swore he saw the handle move. He started toward the door when he heard Jessica yell at him to get back in the interrogation room. Jessica had Bubba cuffed and was leading him out the door. Chet took the handcuffed prisoner and led him away. John and Jessica turned back toward the bleeding brother who was busy eating John's food the best he could with broken teeth. Jessica looked at John in surprise. John just shrugged. He went over, and grabbed the pad that was on the table, and tore away the first sheet that had blood on it. He really hoped Eugene didn't have any blood borne disease.

"You need to write what I tell you," John began, but Jessica interrupted him.

"I'll write it, and he can sign it," Jessica said. Eugene nodded to that and kept right on eating. He winced once when he hit one of his broken teeth on a chicken bone.

"That is absolutely disgusting," Jessica said in a low voice to John.

"It's like a car wreck," John replied in awe and fascination. "I can't look away." Jessica shook her head and began to write. When she finished, she handed the pad to Eugene. He signed, belched, and continued on. The door opened, and Chet led the medical team in along with another agent. They gave Eugene the once over and decided to take Eugene with them. The other agent that had come in with Chet accompanied Eugene and the medical team. Chet, Jessica, and John surveyed the carnage in the room and wondered if their careers were over.

"Trip's going to kill us," Chet moaned. "He's going to split us back up, and we'll never solve this case." Jessica looked around and wondered what, if anything, they could do to get out of this mess.

"Maybe not," John said. "What does Trip love more than anything?"

"You getting shown up," Chet automatically responded. John nodded and turned toward Jessica.

"Do you know any type of wrestling or self-defense moves?" John asked. The smile that crossed Jessica's face made John pause. It was more than a little creepy. "Okay," John said, taking her smile to mean yes. "Here's what we do." The group huddled together to come up with a plan.

John and Jessica's Apartment
Now

Chapter 49

John and Trip were in the kitchen talking, while Jessica was reading the latest manuscript. She finished and came into the kitchen to join them.

"John, something didn't make sense," she said.

"What's that?" John asked.

"You wrote a part that I didn't know and that you didn't address," she said. "You left it hanging."

"Was that the part where Trip almost got caught coming out of the observation room after Eugene got his teeth broke?" John asked, looking at Trip the entire time. Trip almost spit out his drink in surprise. Jessica's mouth dropped open in shock.

"How?" Trip asked, dumbfounded. "How did you figure that one out?"

"I didn't until you told me about your phone conversation with Jeremiah," John admitted. "It was then that a lot of things made sense to me. I never thought about those things back then, but now that I'm reviewing what happened for the book, a few things weren't adding up. I actually plan on taking that part out of the final draft. I just wanted Trip to read it for fun." John's grin was back. Jessica and Trip traded looks.

"Are you sure you want him back when he heals?" Jessica asked. Trip smiled, took a drink, and turned toward Jessica.

"I think the FBI has suffered from the absence of John Fowler long enough," Trip said. John shook his head like he had misheard. He put his little finger in his ear and wiggled it around like he was trying to get something loose. Trip rolled his eyes and took another drink.

"So, I can come back?" John asked hopefully.

"Just as soon as you are medically cleared and . . ." Trip paused, realizing he had talked his way into a corner.

"You were going to say cleared by his wife?" Jessica asked with a smirk on her face. Trip shook his head. "Trip, everyone knows we are married." John turned to her.

"In his mind, he just stuck his fingers in his ears and sang, 'la la la, I can't hear you,'" John said. Trip barked a laugh at that comment.

"Plausible deniability," Trip said with a grin on his face. The three stood there smiling and laughing for a bit until Trip turned serious.

"What's wrong?" John asked.

"It's Chet," Trip admitted. John nodded for Trip to continue. "He and Ron are working on Chet's marksmanship." John couldn't see a problem with that. Trip took a deep breath and continued. "I think Chet believes it's his fault that you got shot."

"That's ridiculous," John said. Trip nodded. John studied Trip; there was something that Trip wasn't telling them. "There's more, isn't there," John said, not asked. Trip nodded again.

"He found out that Bruce isn't in prison," Trip said. John felt the world stop. Nothing seemed to move, but his chest began to hurt. He swore he could feel the bullets tearing through him again. Pain radiated through his chest, and he thought his heart might stop. He put his hand on his chest where the pain radiated from. He looked down in what felt like slow motion. He just knew he was going to see blood flowing over his hand, out of his chest, where the bullets had ripped through him again. He was surprised he wasn't bleeding.

125

"JOHN!" John heard someone yell, and suddenly, time was back to normal. He whipped his head around to Jessica; the look of concern on her face told him he looked like he felt. John looked over at Trip. It didn't take someone with John's ability to see what was on Trip's face. John knew his going back to the FBI was now in serious jeopardy.

Chapter 50

Jessica helped John over to the couch to sit down. Trip sat down in a chair across from him. Trip looked ready to spring up to catch him if anything went wrong. John had never seen Trip look so worried before.

"I'm okay," John said, breathing normally again.

"What was that?" Trip asked.

"PTSD," Jessica said quietly. Trip whipped his head to Jessica, saw she was absolutely serious, and then, he turned to John. John didn't say anything. Jessica was right.

"He was cleared," Trip said.

"It's obviously not debilitating," John said. Trip shook his head. He ran his hand across his head, trying to make sense of what he had just seen. If this was PTSD, then John wasn't as ready for active duty as Trip thought John was.

"Ron warned me," Jessica said quietly.

"I am right here," John growled.

"See, he's moody," Jessica said, trying to lighten the mood. John was glad to see she could find the humor in it.

"Trip, I'm going to have some issues," John admitted. Trip was stunned. He assumed he was going to have to fight John tooth and nail on this one. John continued. "Ron and I have been talking about this. He told me his worries when he started working on this person Jessica and I keep seeing. I want to compromise with you." Trip looked very surprised. Jessica raised an eyebrow and sat down beside him. She had never known John to ever offer up a compromise with anyone. She resisted the urge to check for a fever.

"I want you to let me come back, but I want Ron to stay on the team to watch me," John said. Jessica and Trip exchanged a glance. They both turned back to John. He

127

continued. "If he at any point thinks I'm debilitated by this, he pulls the plug on me being there. I have no say in the matter." Trip barked a laugh.

"You not having a say in the matter has never stopped you before," Trip said. John smiled; he had to agree. "Should you be in therapy?" John shrugged.

"Probably," John admitted. "But, we all know my alcoholism therapy isn't conventional, and frankly, it's what works for me." Trip had to admit John was right. John continued. "I talk to Ron constantly, and I know a lot about what to expect. I expected for this to hit me the first time I saw Bruce or something, but this caught me off-guard." Trip nodded.

"I'm sorry. I didn't know," Trip said.

"How is he not in jail?" John asked. "Where is he?"

"He's in a psychiatric facility against my protests," Trip explained. John nodded. "You're taking this well." John shrugged.

"If he gets out, I get to shoot him again," John explained. Jessica shut her eyes. Trip leaned forward, finger pointing.

"You are not to go on some stupid vendetta again! Do you understand me?" Trip barked.

"He's not out, so calm down," John replied. "I'm just saying if it happens, this time, I'm going to make sure he doesn't come back."

"Don't go there, John," Jessica said, sliding her hand over his. John looked down at her hand and up at her. After a second, he sighed and relented.

"No vendetta," he said simply. Jessica smiled and nodded. John looked back at Trip. "Do we have a deal on my return?" Trip nodded.

"If Ron says you need counseling," Trip began.

"Then, I get counseling," John finished his sentence. "If you two really think I do, then I will. So far, this is the first time anything has happened. I've had trouble sleeping, but I've always had trouble sleeping. I would think my reaction to what I heard would be considered quite natural. I'll even go see someone now and get retested if you think I need to. I know PTSD is nothing to joke about, but this is my first really known symptom if that's what it is."

"You and Ron talked about this at length," Trip said more than asked. John nodded.

"I haven't avoided thinking about it or anything like that," John replied.

"This was one of the reasons you brought Ron onto the investigation of the girl you and Jessica are seeing," Trip stated. John couldn't help himself. He began to grin. Jessica closed her eyes and took a deep breath. John thought she was trying to resist the urge to punch him. "You just can't help yourself some days, can you?" John grinned at Trip and looked over at Jessica. Jessica was looking at him, obviously worried. She wrapped her arms around his arm.

"I'm okay," John said quietly.

"For now," Jessica replied. John rubbed his hand over hers. She smiled at him and nodded. John turned toward Trip.

"If I keep having these reactions, or if you all think I'm getting moodier than usual, then I will go see someone," John offered. Trip thought for a second and nodded.

"You good with that?" Trip asked Jessica. She nodded. "Are you okay?"

"No," she admitted. "Why didn't you tell me about Bruce?"

"I wanted him better before everyone found out," Trip said, nodding his head toward John. "Besides, I kept thinking I could get Bruce back into prison, but it's pretty

129

obvious by now it's not going to happen. When the Vice President of the United States says someone needs to go to jail, and he still goes to a psychiatric facility instead…well, there's not much you can do." John started laughing.

"It's bad when your own dad tries to get you locked up," John said. The three talked for a bit, and Trip bid them good night. Jessica got ready for bed, while John went to the living room window and looked out. He didn't hear Jessica behind him and jumped when he felt her hand on his shoulder.

"What are you thinking about?" she asked. John never turned around; he just continued to look out the window.

"That was absolutely terrifying," John admitted. "I can't imagine what some of these poor souls go through." Jessica hugged him from behind. John put his hand over hers.

"You coming to bed?" she asked. John shook his head.

"I can't sleep," John admitted. Jessica squeezed him tighter.

"Come on, I'll read you a bedtime story," Jessica said, laughing. John turned around and put his arm around her, and they headed to the bedroom together.

"Will you read me the one where he says, 'the game is afoot'?" John asked.

"Do you ever not think about mysteries?" Jessica asked. John shook his head.

"It's what makes me, me," he admitted. Jessica smiled at him.

"I guess I wouldn't want you any other way," she admitted. Deep down, she was worried though. What would happen the first time John was in a shooting? What would she do the first time John was in a shooting?

John Fowler
8 Years Ago

Chapter 51

John stared out the window at the passing scenery thinking about the conversation at the FBI. Trip had decided it would be easier to take the prisoner by car to the location of the second bomb.

"Shouldn't we have a bomb squad there?" John asked.

"Is it armed?" Trip asked. John looked at Eugene.

"Nope," Eugene replied. "In fact, only Bubba and I know where it is, so no one else can get to it." John felt his heart sink. He turned back to Trip who had a satisfied smile on his face.

"Anything else?" Trip asked.

"Doesn't this place sound like a place out of that paranormal show about the FBI?" Chet asked. John and Trip turned to look at Chet, almost in disgust. Chet raised his hands.

"It was a good show!" he exclaimed, defending himself.

"It is near where that show was supposed to be on one of those episodes," Eugene answered. "But, they got things all wrong." Trip nodded.

"Sounds good to me," Trip replied.

"Why in a car?" John almost whined.

"Do you want to deal with him on a flight?" Trip asked, pointing at Eugene. Eugene gave John a smile that creeped John out from all the missing teeth Eugene had as a result of Bubba Ray's fist. "Besides, you hate flying."
John sighed. Jessica had taken the keys from the start, and she was driving them through the states of New York, New

Jersey, Pennsylvania, Maryland, West Virginia, Virginia, and finally Tennessee.

"Only about 200 miles to go," Jessica announced as they entered Tennessee.

"Are you going to drive the whole way?" John asked.

"I don't see why not," Jessica answered. Chet snickered from the back seat.

"What are you laughing about?" John asked, half irritated.

"You two," Chet answered. "If I didn't know better, I'd swear you two were married." Jessica and John glanced at each other at the exact same time. They quickly looked straight ahead at the road in front of them.

"What's wrong with them?" Eugene asked from the back seat.

"Shut up!" Jessica and John both snapped together. They quickly exchanged looks again and then looked straight ahead, not daring to even acknowledge each other. Chet sat in the back, shaking his head. A few miles later, they stopped at a rest area. Chet and John took Eugene to the bathroom, and when they got back, Jessica was still gone. They got Eugene in the car, and Chet decided to talk to his friend.

Chapter 52

Chet turned toward John after shutting Eugene in the car.

"John, what's wrong?" Chet asked.

"What do you mean?" John asked, trying to think of a way to avoid the discussion Chet wanted to have.

"You and Jessica, what is going on?" Chet asked.

"Are you implying that I would cheat on Sam?" John asked, getting angry.

"No," Chet replied simply. "If there is anyone who I could say would never cheat on his wife, it's you." John nodded, anger leaving his face. He looked over at the interstate for a minute and the traffic going back and forth. When he turned back to Chet, confusion was evident on his face.

"There's something about her," John admitted softly like he was actually admitting things to himself. "She drives me absolutely crazy and not in a good way. It's like she challenges me at every step, she's...maddening. That's what she is." Chet said nothing. He knew his friend needed to talk. John continued. "I mean she's attractive, but I've met attractive people before. I don't get it, Chet. She's nothing like Sam. Sam's the only person who has really understood me, but Jessica...she seems to as well, but it's different. You know?" Chet nodded, and John began to chuckle. "I really have no idea what I'm saying."

"You weren't what they called a ladies' man in your youth, were you?" Chet asked. John looked away but shook his head slightly. "It is possible to be friends with someone you find attractive." John brought his head around quickly to retort but saw the seriousness on Chet's face. He slowly nodded.

"I don't know what to do," John admitted. "I don't know how to deal with these types of situations. Always before, if I didn't know how to deal with something, I'd just ignore it, and for the most part, it would just go away. I guess that's why I have so few friends." Chet looked at John sympathetically. He couldn't imagine what it was like to be John.

"Just be yourself," Chet said. "Don't ignore her, but just be yourself, and say whatever you would normally say."

"What are you two so deep in conversation about?" Jessica asked. John and Chet hadn't noticed her approach. John turned toward Jessica and decided to take Chet's advice and be himself. That meant John needed to be truthful.

"Chet and I were discussing your hotness, and what I'm going to do about it," John answered. Jessica stared straight at John, not sure how to respond. After a second or so, John realized he had messed up.

"I'm going to have to go to more training, aren't I?" John asked. Jessica slowly nodded, and then to John's surprise, she smiled warmly at him.

"That was a good one, Fowler," Jessica said as she opened the door to get in the car. "I didn't know you had that kind of sense of humor." Jessica got in the car and shut the door. John turned to his friend, confused. Chet quickly shook his head and mouthed, "Go with it." John was so confused.

"Can you two get in now? We'll have a slumber party later for you two to discuss your lack of love lives," Jessica said from the car. John opened the door, irritated, and got in.

"You know I'm married, right?" John asked. Jessica nodded.

"That woman deserves sainthood for marrying you," Jessica replied.

"I've never heard her complain," John answered, smugly.

"That would require you to quit thinking about how great you are, and try listening for a change," Jessica replied, backing the car out. Chet made a hissing noise in the backseat. John turned toward his friend.

"You're not helping," John replied.

"And, we all know you need all the help you can get," Jessica replied.

"You sure you two aren't married?" Eugene asked. Jessica stopped the car, put it in park, and turned toward Eugene.

"Listen," Jessica began, more than a little irritated. "What John and I do is none of your business. If I hate him or have a burning desire that keeps me up nights for him, it is none of your business."

"It's the latter of the two," John said. Jessica turned around, put the car in drive, and headed back to the interstate. She glanced over at John.

"You wish," she retorted. John looked over and grinned at her. Jessica rolled her eyes. "She definitely deserves sainthood." The four continued their ride down the road.

Chapter 53

Jessica pulled up to the spot where her GPS told her to go, and all she saw was a field. She turned to Eugene.

"I guess the GPS is off," she said. "Where do I need to go?" Eugene smiled and shrugged. Jessica's eyes narrowed. "Eugene, where do we need to go?" she asked more forcefully. John watched the exchange and decided this was one of those moments that weren't covered in the handbook. He got out of the car, walked around to the door, yanked it opened, and pulled Eugene out of the car. Chet and Jessica both rushed out of the car. John grabbed Eugene by the shirt collar.

"I know you think this is cute and funny, but right now, we need to know where that bomb is. Do you understand me?" The look on John's face was of complete seriousness. Chet walked over, grabbed John, and pulled him away from Eugene.

"You can't do this," Chet said with panic on his face. "He has rights!"

"So do the people that could die if that bomb goes off," John retorted.

"John, if you do this, your career is over," Chet said desperately.

"If I don't, lives could be over," John replied. He pushed past his friend, pulled his weapon, and pointed it at Eugene. "Where?" he asked quietly. Eugene laughed.

"You ain't got the clip in, you idiot," Eugene said. Jessica groaned and rolled her eyes.

"Is this your two's version of good cop, bad cop?" she asked. John turned to Jessica.

"I'm sorry," John replied. "Do you have any other great ideas?"

"Actually, I do," Jessica replied. She came around the car and grabbed Eugene by the shoulder. She spun him around, and he was looking at the shinny roof of the car.

"What do you see?" she asked very quietly.

"My reflection," Eugene answered.

"Good," Jessica replied. "I want you to remember what you looked like. Remember. This is all on you." With that, she slammed Eugene's face on the roof of the car. Eugene's face bounced, and he stumbled backwards. Blood began gushing down his nose. John and Chet were frozen in shock. Jessica turned toward Eugene and began advancing toward him as he stumbled backwards. She pulled her gun and fired just over Eugene's left shoulder. Eugene screamed and fell back.

"Where? Is? The? BOMB?" she asked.

"I ain't ever telling you, you crazy -" Eugene began screaming. He never finished his sentence as Jessica pointed her gun at Eugene and fired her weapon.

John's and Jessica's Apartment
Now

Chapter 54

Jessica laid the manuscript down on the table. She turned toward John with a slightly ashamed look on her face. John was trying to keep a straight face but was losing a battle with his grin.

"You ever wonder what he was going to call me?" Jessica asked as seriously as she could.

"I have a pretty good idea," John admitted, completely losing the battle with the grin. Jessica grabbed the throw pillow on the couch beside her and hit John with it. John barely tried to defend himself. Jessica, with amusement on her face, just threw the pillow at John, got up from the couch, and began to walk behind it. She put both her hands over her face. She pushed her palms over her temple and on through her hair.

"I was horrible back then," Jessica said.

"At the way you treated suspects, or the way you shamelessly flirted with your partner?" John asked. Jessica stuck her tongue out at John.

"Hush," she said, half serious. She turned and began to walk to the kitchen. John got up and followed her. She got a glass of water and took a drink, leaning against the wall facing John.

"I had no idea how pitiful you were with women back then," Jessica said, holding the glass with both hands. "I assumed you knew I would never, ever act on anything. You know, after the whole Tennessee fiasco, I told Sam everything. I mean everything. All of our barbs, jabs, and me trying to hit you," Jessica admitted.

"Oh, thanks, I had almost forgotten to add that," John said, looking for something to write with. Jessica shook her head and rolled her eyes as John scribbled notes onto a napkin. He finished and turned back to Jessica, giving her his full attention. Jessica took another drink and stared at John for a second before continuing.

"I thought she would be furious," Jessica said, slightly smiling while playing the memory in her mind. "I remember her laughing hysterically and saying, 'I bet he was so flabbergasted that he didn't know what to say and just told you the truth.' I didn't know what she was talking about until I read the part about you having to go for more harassment training." John smiled.

"You know, there were days Chet and I just couldn't stand you," John said seriously. Jessica laughed out loud.

"Someone had to break up your little boys' club," Jessica replied, still laughing. "Besides, I really don't think either of you took all the classes you were supposed to." John didn't answer, but the smile on his face was answer enough. "I know I was way too over the top back then," Jessica admitted. "But," she said, pointing her finger at John. "You two were doing whatever you wanted and saying whatever you wanted." John nodded.

"Why shouldn't we?" John asked. Jessica couldn't believe what she was hearing. John raised his hand in defense. "You understand you were the first person to be able to work with us. Actually, let me correct that. You were the first person to be able to work with me. Chet and I had worked together from time to time, but there were times that he begged out of working with me before you showed up. You were the missing piece that made us all click. Besides, you know we all looked out for each other." Jessica smiled.

"Why didn't you have me fired?" Jessica asked.

139

"For what you did in Tennessee?" John asked, and Jessica nodded. "Because what you said was true. Lives were at stake, and he was playing a game. Besides, I'm not entirely sure if you hadn't done what you did, we would have ever found out what we needed in time."

"But, you covered it up!" Jessica exclaimed. John began to grin. Jessica shook her head. Her body betrayed her and a grin of her own began to grow across her face. She knew the words that came out of John's mouth before he said them.

"Nah," John said. "I just told a certain version of the truth."

Tennessee
8 Years Ago

Chapter 55

John was staring at the bloody mess that was Eugene. John's heart was pumping in his chest as he looked at their prisoner. Blood was now coming down Eugene's eyes from the scratches and cuts in his forehead where the dirt and gravel that Jessica had shot had kicked up. Eugene was still staring at a spot in the ground, just inches from the crotch in his blue jeans. If John was pressed, he would have to admit the crotch of Eugene's pants did look damp.

"Where is it?" Jessica asked very quietly, leveling the gun at Eugene's head. John stepped forward, took the gun away from Jessica, and tossed it to Chet.

"What are you doing!?" Jessica screamed. John put his hand in her face and ignored her. Jessica wasn't for sure whether to be mad at the gesture or laugh at how absurd he looked right then.

"Eugene. Eugene, look at me!" John shouted. Eugene looked up at John. Eugene appeared to be in complete shock. "Game's over, Eugene; I'll give her the gun back if you don't answer me." Eugene murmured something and turned and pointed.

"Oh, great, he's so scared he can't speak," John muttered. He turned to talk to Jessica. It was at that moment, out of the corner of his eye, he saw Jessica ball her fist and take a swing. John moved out of the way just in the nick of time. Eugene looked like he was ready to cry. John stumbled while avoiding the punch and fell to the ground. Jessica stood over him, looking like she was ready to pounce on him and do some serious damage to John.

Chet ran up and tried to pull Jessica back, and she just shrugged him off.

"Take care of Eugene, Chet," John said, staring daggers at Jessica. "I'll take care of this." John got to his feet, while Chet helped Eugene up and led him to the car to treat his wounds. Jessica walked up to John, less than an inch separated their noses.

"Who do you think you are?" she asked very quietly, almost dangerously.

"I'm the guy who kept you from getting fired," John replied just as quietly. Tension filled the air.

"You really think I would have shot him?" Jessica asked.

"It doesn't matter," John answered. "He thought you were going to, and that's terrorism."

"That's bull, and you know it!" Jessica spat.

"You have no clue how close you came to throwing away your entire career in the FBI!" John hissed. Jessica crossed her arms in front of her, almost challenging John. "Look at him!" John pointed at Eugene. Jessica looked at Eugene and then at John. John pointed again. "Look at him," he said calmly, but fiercely. "He's done nothing wrong."

"He could have led to the death of hundreds, if not thousands, of people by not telling us where the second bomb is," Jessica answered, anger welling up in her again.

"And, if we resort to the tactics you used, what does that make us? The good guys or the bad guys?" John asked. Jessica stared at John. Anger slowly left her face. She glanced over at Eugene and then looked back at John. A look of shame was on her face. "Go clean him up, and we'll stop this bomb." John turned away from her. Jessica stood there for a second, but either John didn't realize she was still there or just ignored her. Jessica went back to the car to clean up Eugene. Chet left her with Eugene after assuring Eugene that Jessica wasn't armed. Chet walked up to John.

"Went kinda hard on her, boss," Chet said, more than asked.

"She can't cross the line," John answered, never turning toward Chet.

"You were ready to cross the line, weren't you," Chet said, more than asked again. John chuckled and turned toward his friend. A grin covered John's face.

"I don't know if I'm upset with her for doing what she did or myself for thinking it was exactly the right call in this situation," John admitted quietly to his friend. Chet nodded.

"What happens when you cross that line?" Chet asked rhetorically. John looked at Chet, shrugged, and shook his head.

"I hope we never have to find out," John admitted, looking over at the car and wondering what they were going to find with this second bomb.

Chapter 56

"We've found the supposed site," John told Trip over Chet's cell phone.

"Everything okay?" Trip asked. John glanced over at Jessica and Eugene. Jessica still had a challenging look on her face. John shook his head.

"Eugene took a nasty spill and got himself all cut up," John said. "I think he saw something that scared him, and Jessica fired off a couple of shots to scare something. He was so scared he couldn't talk. Who knows what he saw? I think it scared Eugene and he managed to wet his pants." John swore he heard muffled laughter on the other end, but Trip sounded business-like when he spoke next.

"Find that bomb, and try not to get killed," Trip replied.

"I'll do my best on both accounts, sir," John replied. The line was already dead. John looked at the phone. "Love you too, Trip," he said sarcastically at the phone. John handed the phone over to Chet.

"Looks like it's time for us to find this bomb," John said to his two partners. Jessica stared at him icily. John couldn't help but grin. "Cheer up, Jessica. You may get your wish, and this bomb could blow up, taking me with you."

"I don't want to see you dead, John," Jessica replied sweetly. John was a little surprised with the sudden kindness and started to give her a grateful smile. He started to . . . until Jessica continued. "If you're dead, I won't be able to torment you. No, I much prefer you stuck in a wheelchair for the rest of your life." With that, she grabbed Eugene and started toward the area he had pointed to earlier. Eugene looked at John and Chet as if to say, "Help." John shrugged and grinned at Eugene's predicament. Chet leaned closely where Jessica couldn't hear him.

144

"She's got a special kind of hate for you," Chet said quietly.

"What can I say? Women love me," John replied. Chet couldn't help but chuckle.

"You are a true ladies' man," Chet replied. John turned toward his friend.

"Thing is, she's probably right about the whole thing," John admitted. "We can't let this bomb go off."

"Yeah with the events of 9/11, the last thing this country needs is to believe there is another terrorist cell running around," Chet said. John stared at Chet blankly.

"I was just thinking we don't want any innocent people to die," John said. Chet's face colored with a slightly red hue. "But, there is what you said to consider as well," John added, trying to lessen his friend's embarrassment.

"Are you two ladies going to gossip all day or help me find this bomb?" Jessica yelled at them. John turned toward Jessica and Eugene. He didn't think anyone could be more irritating than Jessica.

"She's going to make an unlucky someone very miserable one day," John said to Chet. Chet chuckled.

"It's a good thing you're married," Chet replied. John, shock covering his face, turned to look at his friend. Chet shrugged. "You like her. Just admit it." John was astonished.

"What do you mean I like her?" he asked. "She's bullheaded, stubborn, a pain in my backside, and makes me want to pull my hair out." Chet interrupted.

"First off," Chet began with a huge smile on his face. "You've used three words to describe the same thing. Secondly, you once described Sam the same way, and thirdly, it's okay to like someone, John. You can't help who you like and who you don't like. What you can do is not act on it. And I have no doubt that you would never do

145

anything inappropriate. I mean it's not just in your DNA to do something like that. Just admit it, John. You like her." John set his jaw and turned to look at Jessica who had her arms crossed, staring at the two men.

"I mean, seriously, do you two want to break out a tea set and sit and chat!?" Jessica yelled at them. John turned toward Chet.

"You must think I have some sort of death wish," John said. He began to walk toward Jessica and Eugene. "I don't care if Sam wasn't around. There is no way I would ever be with her. She's twenty-five pounds of crazy in a five pound bag, and I don't need that in my life!"

John's and Jessica's Apartment
Now

Chapter 57

Ron and John were sitting in the living room talking when laughter burst out of the bedroom. Ron, not sure what was going on, gave John a strange look. John smiled and waved it away like it wasn't important.

"Jessica is reading the newest part of the manuscript," John said. Ron nodded like he understood, but he really didn't. "She loves reading this old story for some reason. I guess so much has changed; it's good to look back at where we came from and see how much we've grown. I think she enjoys knowing how much I claimed I didn't want to have a relationship with her, and now, we're married." John shook his head, half annoyed with the whole book thing and then changed the subject. "So, you think this will work?"

"If you're right about what you've told me, I think this is our best course of action," Ron replied. John nodded, impressed.

"If I didn't know you were ex-military, I would now after that plan," John said with a smile. Ron chuckled. "How's it going in the office?" Ron looked up, surprised.

"What do you mean?" Ron asked.

"I mean, how is it going? Are you clearing any cases?" John asked. Ron nodded.

"We've cleared three bank robberies," Ron replied. John shuddered.

"There's nothing more I hate than dealing with bank robberies," John admitted. He paused. "Okay, I hate kidnappings first and then bank robberies."

"Interesting," Ron replied. "You've managed to miss them in your time off." John smiled.

"I guess that's the silver lining they're always talking about," John replied. Jessica walked into the room and whacked John in the shoulder with the current manuscript.

"I love it!" she said, continuing across the room to a chair. John rubbed his arm.

"I'd hate to see what you'd do to me if you hated it," John said. Ron shook his head.

"Have you two always been so...violent?" he asked. Jessica nodded.

"I think I could claim spousal abuse," John said, half-serious.

"You like it," Jessica said.

"Not quite as much as you like to think I do," John replied.

"You big baby," Jessica said. Ron stood.

"Okay, I'm going to go before you two start," Ron said. "I've already went through the plan with Jessica. Let me know if we need to change anything." John nodded.

"Thanks again, Ron," John said, extending his hand as he stood. Ron shook it, nodded at Jessica, and left the apartment. John turned toward Jessica.

"It's time to end this mess," John said.

"Agreed," Jessica said. She picked up the manuscript, shoved it in his chest, patted his cheek, and headed into the kitchen.

"That's not what I meant!" John yelled to the kitchen where Jessica ignored him. "I've got to finish this thing if it kills me," John said to himself. "And, it just might."

Tennessee
8 Years Ago

Chapter 58

Eugene led the three agents to a mound of earth that didn't look any different than any other part of the field.

"There," he said, gesturing toward it. "Brother Jones and the others will be in there."

"Jones?" Chet asked, color draining from his face. Chet reached for his weapon. Jessica looked confused. John gave her a look to keep silent.

"Chet, it doesn't mean he's any part of Jim Jones and Jonesville," John said, trying to keep his friend calm. John could see understanding on Jessica's face. She hesitated and then drew her weapon as well. John gave her a look.

"Rather safe than sorry," she replied. John signed and felt the mound of earth where Eugene had pointed to and felt a door. He began to work his hand around to find a handle.

"I know what you're thinking, John," Chet said.

"That this leader and Jim Jones have the same last name and that there is a massive conspiracy?" John asked. John couldn't see Chet's face, but he could tell from the expression on Jessica's that he had nailed it. "Not everything is a conspiracy, Chet."

"You think he wants to kill all of us?" Eugene asked. John continued to dig in the earth. "Brother Jones wouldn't hurt anyone."

"I wish we had done some background work on this Brother Jones before we left," Chet said. John and Jessica shared a quick glance. They both had to agree with Chet on that thought. They should have done more background, but the bomb had seemed to cloud everyone's judgment.

"Would of, could of," John said as he turned the handle, opening the door covered with earth. John had to admit he was impressed. He turned and faced his team. "Next time," he promised. Neither Chet nor Jessica looked comforted by that thought.

"Is there anything worse than cultists?" Chet asked.

"Bank robberies," John answered and started down the stairway he had uncovered. Jessica and Chet exchanged glances, shrugged and continued after John. They both jumped back as John's head appeared out of the stairwell. "Kidnappings," he added. "I hate kidnappings," and with that, he disappeared again.

"I almost shot him," Jessica said, her heart beating a hundred beats a minute from the fright.

"Is that from the fright, or you just almost shot him?" Chet asked. Jessica stopped, turned toward Chet, and smiled.

"I'm not really sure," Jessica admitted. "You'll watch my six?" she asked. Chet nodded, and Jessica headed inside. Chet waved Eugene in.

"What does 'watch my six mean'?" Eugene asked.

"Watch her back," Chet explained. Eugene smiled.

"I'll gladly watch it for her," Eugene said, suggestively. Chet cocked his gun, and Eugene hurried down the stairway. Chet looked around.

"I hate cults," he said and disappeared into the ground.

Chapter 59

John headed down the stairway to the bottom. When he got there, he saw a light switch and turned it on. Lights popped on, and John realized he was in a compound that had to extend for what seemed like miles. He gave a low whistle. John decided to wait on the team before going ahead. It wasn't to protect them or anything like that; he was just worried he might get lost. Jessica, then Eugene, and finally Chet made it to the bottom of the stairwell. Chet let out a similar low whistle.

"What is this place?" Chet asked.

"It's our bunker for doomsday," Eugene said.

"It's pretty big for just a few people," John said. Eugene looked at John questioningly. "There doesn't appear to be anyone around," John said, waving his hand toward the empty hallway. Eugene scratched his face, confusion evident on his face.

"Where is everyone?" he asked. Eugene turned toward John. Panic covered Eugene's face. "Where are they?" John shook his head.

"I don't know," John replied. He was beginning to get worried. "Where's the biggest room?"

"It's this way," Eugene replied and set off toward the way he gestured. "The kitchen has the most space." He turned toward John. "You don't think they're dead do you?"

"Why would you think that?" John asked. "Do you think there would be a mass suicide?" Eugene shook his head.

"No," he replied. "No, I'm sure there wouldn't be." John was worried. He thought Eugene was trying to convince himself more than he was John or the rest of the team. Eugene started to pick up pace. John turned toward his partners and pulled his weapon. The other two nodded, and all four picked up the pace as they hurried down the hall. They turned a corner, and John saw double doors with a chain running though the handles with a lock on it, effectively locking anyone behind the doors inside.

"Are there any other doors into this room?" John asked. Eugene nodded.

"There are at least three other doorways," he admitted. John stepped in front of Eugene, turned toward Jessica who had her gun drawn.

"How good a shot are you?" he asked quietly.

"Good enough to take down seven or eight before they get on you," she replied. John nodded.

"Let's hope that will do the trick," he replied to her quietly. He turned toward the door, took a deep breath, and yelled out as loud as he could. "This is John Fowler of the FBI. Drop any weapons you might have! Step away from the door! We are going to shoot the lock off!" John listened and didn't hear anything. He turned back to Jessica. The look in her eyes mirrored the feelings he was having in his gut. The only thing that didn't have him in a complete panic was he didn't smell anything. He hoped there was a good reason for that. Jessica nodded at him. John turned, took a deep breath, and fired two shots at the lock, watching it fall away from the chains holding the door shut. He walked forward, pulled the chain down, took a deep breath, and threw the doors open.

Bruce Cosby
Now

Chapter 60

Bruce looked up as he heard a commotion at his door. Four orderlies were making their way into his room. They had Bruce stand. Bruce smiled as he stood and was shackled and chained, which was odd. He was supposed to be in a psychiatric hospital, not a prison. He had an idea what was going on, and he was more than a little amused by it.

"No face mask, guys?" he asked, causing the orderlies to pause just a second. Bruce laughed maniacally. He figured why hold back everything he felt inside? He was in the hospital because someone, somewhere, had signed off on him being mentally unwell, and he hated to disappoint people. Bruce found that idea funny and continued his laughter as he was led down the hallway. He was taken to an elevator. He began to wonder if he was being freed by his friend. He didn't think this would be how it happened, but who knew? When the elevator doors opened, he knew it wasn't his friend's escape plan but instead, a meeting--a meeting with a very important man that Bruce couldn't decide if he wanted to kill or not.

There were several secret service agents with guns aimed at Bruce as he exited the elevator. He walked as calmly as he could with his feet cuffed. There was no sense taking a bullet over a misunderstanding. Bullets hurt, and the fewer of them Bruce took the better. Bruce was taken by the agents and led down a long hallway to a room. He was unshackled and cuffed to restraints on the table in front of him and the floor.

"Really, guys, is all of this necessary?" he asked.

"I think you should know I am against this entire meeting, but I do what my boss tells me to," one secret service agent replied. He seemed to be the leader of the group. "I also think you know, but just in case you don't, if you look at me or anyone else the wrong way, I won't think twice about taking you out like the rabid dog you are."

"I like you," Bruce said, smiling sickly. He swore he saw the agent involuntarily shiver. Bruce's smile grew. "At least you're man enough to admit what you feel. You need to come play for my team." The agent pulled his hand back like he was about to backhand Bruce and probably would have if a voice hadn't cut through the air.

"Don't" the voice shouted. A man entered the room behind Bruce. Bruce never turned his head. He knew the voice the second he heard it.

"So, now you decide to save me?" Bruce asked, bitterly.

"Save you? Save you? My boy, I just don't want to see anyone else be drug down by your good for nuthin' carcass," the voice answered. Bruce slightly turned his head to see his father come into the room. "You boys can leave me. If there are any problems, I'll take care of them. Personally." Bruce nearly giggled.

"Oooh," Bruce said, trying to mimic fright the best he could while chained. "Are you going to get the paddle out, Daddy?"

"Boy, I'll never forgive myself for not switchin' you more regular!" Jeremiah exclaimed. Bruce sat up the best he could, his eyes dancing.

"Well, come on out behind the woodshed, Dad!" Bruce almost screamed. "But, be warned! It's not me about to take the switching, it's you, you old fool!"

Chapter 61

Jeremiah waved everyone out of the room and waited until the door was shut.

"Now, what are you yammering on about this time, boy?" Jeremiah asked.

"You might want to make sure they're not listening in," Bruce said, trying to act like he was doing Jeremiah a favor.

"They're not listening. They know better," Jeremiah replied, losing his patience.

"It's your funeral," Bruce said, shrugging his shoulders. He smiled, a smile John had often described as what a snake would look like if one could smile. He spoke in a very low voice. "I know."

"What do you know?" Jeremiah asked, unsure what his deranged son was talking about this time. Bruce's smile grew. He was about to make his father very sick inside, and the thought of that made him absolutely giddy. Bruce looked so very proud of himself.

"I. Know," he said as he leaned back and tried to get as comfortable as one could while chained like he was.

"Tarnation, boy!" Jeremiah exclaimed. "What do you think you know!?"

"About the president," Bruce said, watching his father's face. There! He had seen it. For just a second, something flashed across his father's face. He wasn't sure if it was fear, or doubt, or what, but it was definitely something. All those hours of studying facial expressions had paid off. He was no John Fowler at it, but he had caught it. The thought of John led to thoughts of murder, and for a second, Bruce was distracted. Then, he remembered he was torturing his father, and he smiled.

"What about the president?" Jeremiah asked as calmly as he could.

"I know how he did it, and I know what he did," Bruce smiled, feeling giddy inside. He now understood why John loved what he did so much. There was nothing more satisfying than seeing someone try to remain calm, but ultimately break.

"I don't know what you're talking about, my boy," Jeremiah responded. "Have they amped up your medicine?" Bruce smiled, giggled, and leaned forward as much as he could.

"Harrison told me everything," Bruce said in an almost whisper. Color drained from his father's face. Bruce had kept Harrison's secret because Bruce thought Harrison had been an ally. Bruce now knew that Harrison had played him by feeding him the information about Sam being his illegitimate sister. Bruce didn't have any qualms about killing Sam. It was just the being used part that Bruce was upset about. Bruce stared at his father. Jeremiah looked sick to his stomach. Bruce continued in the same low tone.

"And, now, I know that you know, and you haven't told anyone. I know that you, Mr. Truth, Justice, Apple Pie, and The American Way are holding back a secret from the American people. What I also know that no one else knows is that it's killing you inside. You want to tell the truth so bad, but you know how many people it will bring down that you think are fighting the good fight." Jeremiah looked like he might pass out at any moment. Bruce was absolutely right about everything he had just said. Bruce chuckled. He decided to add in one last dig. "And, they call me evil," Bruce added, giggling. Jeremiah slammed his hand on the table, making Bruce smile even more.

"Boy, you know nothing!" Jeremiah exclaimed. "We have dug that evil rat's nest out of the White House. We are doing what we said we would do for the American people. Telling them anything would do nothing but upset them for no good reason!"

"So, you admit it?" Bruce asked softly. Jeremiah froze. "Dad, you just admitted you lied to the American people for their own good. What makes you any better than all the rest?" Bruce let that question hang in the air like an ax over Jeremiah's head. Jeremiah looked like he could cry.

"Here's what we're going to do," Bruce said calmly. "I'm never going to prison, and you're going to make sure that happens, or I'm going to tell everything, and it's going to bring you down. Do you understand me?" Jeremiah sat there in shock.

Chapter 62

Jeremiah sat quietly looking at his son and wondered where it had all gone wrong. What had he done or not done to this boy? What made Bruce this cold, calculating monster? Bruce was smiling and looking very proud of himself.

"Dad, do we understand each other?" Bruce asked, nearly giggling. Jeremiah couldn't speak but slowly nodded.

"We need to use our words," Bruce said, egging his father on. Jeremiah gave Bruce a look of hate that Bruce didn't know his father was capable of. Bruce didn't think he could be any happier than he was right at that second. "Say it."

"I understand," Jeremiah said quietly. Bruce chuckled and leaned in close.

"Welcome to the dark side," Bruce said quietly, and then, he burst into a fit of laughter. Jeremiah stared at him for a second, got up, and knocked on the door. The door opened up seconds later. "My son is ready to go back to his room," Jeremiah said quietly. Secret Service personnel came in, unlocked Bruce from the restraints, and began to lead him away.

"Nice seeing you again, Dad," Bruce said as he passed in front of Jeremiah. Jeremiah turned to look at his son. Bruce broke out into laughter again and went out the door. Jeremiah went back over to the table and sat back down. One of the agents stuck his head in the door.

"Are you ready, sir?" he asked. Jeremiah looked up at him and waved him off.

"I need just a second, okay?" Jeremiah said. The agent left Jeremiah by himself. Jeremiah pulled out a cell phone and looked at it for a minute. He sighed and dialed a number. A voice on the other end answered.

"Bruce knows," Jeremiah simply said. There was complete silence. "Susan, did you hear me?"

"I heard you, Jeremiah," Susan replied.

"I'm so sorry, Susan," Jeremiah said.

"I'm not worried, Jeremiah," Susan replied. "In fact, I feel relief. Let it all come out."

"I don't know if this is the time yet, Susan," Jeremiah replied. "What good will it do?"

"It would end my burden," Susan replied. Jeremiah thought for a second.

"You know the president will never let it happen," Jeremiah responded.

"I could care less about how he feels," Susan snapped. "It's time."

"Susan, what you and your husband did was wrong, but it wasn't like you did it for the reason Kenneth did," Jeremiah replied. "Tarnation! If Bruce tells the entire country, then it will destroy the party, and everything all of us fought for will end. How is that helping? John wouldn't abuse this knowledge. That's why I had no problem asking you if we could tell him, but it never happened due to his accident."

"Do what you think is right, Jeremiah," Susan replied. "But, think about this. If we're keeping secrets, then what makes us better than all of those we set out to stop? What make us right and them wrong? The answer is we're currently in power, and they're not. Think about it, Jeremiah. I trust you to do what's best." And, with that, Susan hung up.

Jeremiah sat in the room and just stared at his phone for several minutes. Then, he stood, straightened his coat, and went out the door. He had a decision to make, one that could end many political careers, possibly even his.

"I never thought things would be this hard," Jeremiah mumbled to himself. "I just thought it would be clear what was right and what was wrong." He headed to his helicopter to head back to Washington, D.C. There, he and the president would talk. After that, who knew?

Tennessee
8 Years Ago

Chapter 63

"Praise Jesus!" The shouts came from the room
that John had just opened the door to. John looked into the
room and saw nearly 100 people, all alive. John said a
silent prayer of thanks. Jessica walked up beside John.

"We get lucky?" she said in a low voice. John
glanced over at her, noticing the relief that covered her
face.

"I don't know," John replied in the same low tone.
"See how much food is here and if there are any weapons.
We don't need any surprises." Jessica nodded and began to
work her way over to a group of women who rushed to hug
Jessica. John had little time to enjoy the discomfort Jessica
was experiencing. A man approached him.

"I am Allen Jones. Some refer to me as Brother
AJ," the man said, extending his hand. John shook his
hand; it would have been rude not to. Plus, there was the
fact they were outnumbered 100 to 3, and he really didn't
want to cause any problems if there wasn't any reason.
Whether or not John agreed with these people and what
they were doing, as long as they weren't hurting anyone, it
wasn't his place to interfere with them.

"I'd like to welcome you to the Temple of Light and
Hope," Brother AJ said. "While I am very thankful for you
saving us, I am also a little bothered by what appears to be
FBI agents on our property, holding one of our flock in
cuffs. He also appears to be injured."

"I apologize, sir," John responded. "My name is
John Fowler, and I am an FBI agent. Your flock member,
Eugene, and his friend Bubba Ray were found to be in

possession of a bomb in New York City." Shock covered AJ's face. John continued. "They told me that there was another bomb in this area, and that's why we are here." AJ shook his head sadly.

"I was afraid of this," Brother AJ replied. "Mr. Fowler, I give you access to this entire compound to search for any clue you might need to find this bomb."

"Sir," John began.

"How about just AJ?" AJ said with a smile. John nodded.

"AJ, we were told the bomb is actually here in this compound," John said.

"If that's the case shouldn't we evacuate the building?" AJ asked, looking concerned. John hadn't actually thought about that. He had been so concerned in protecting innocents that he had failed to take into account that the people living here could be innocent. John, slightly ashamed of himself, nodded.

"Jessica," he yelled. She looked up at him in surprise. "We need to evacuate everyone." Jessica nodded and began leading people to the exit. Chet was already helping a group of children to calmly exit the building. John turned to AJ. "Is there anyone that isn't in this room?"

"The only people that weren't here were Eugene, Bubba, and Brad," AJ said.

"Who's Brad?" John asked.

"The man that locked us in the room," AJ answered. "Mr. Fowler, I have no problem answering any of your questions, but don't you think we had best evacuate everyone else first?" John nodded. He and AJ checked all the rooms on their way out to make sure that no one had been left behind. Once they got above ground, AJ made a quick count to make sure everyone was accounted for. Jessica came over to John while the count was taking place.

"Learn anything?" she asked in a low voice.

"I learned some guy named Brad chained them all in there, but that's as far as I got," John said quietly. "He seems to be cooperative so far."

"I've seen no sign of abuse in any of the children," Jessica said. "I did talk to one mother and asked her if her children had done anything weird in school. She admitted that one schoolteacher, a Mr. Smith, had them write some strange things, but he tried to assure everyone it was just an exercise to practice writing. And before you ask, Mr. Smith isn't here anymore."

"What do you want to bet this Brad and Mr. Smith are the same person?" John asked. Jessica nodded, already having the same thought.

"We need to check that compound," Jessica said. John looked over at the group that had gathered away from the compound entrance.

"You do realize that if one of them has a trigger, and we're down there . . . ." John trailed off with his thoughts. He looked at Jessica and saw on her face she had been thinking the same thing.

Chapter 64

"There's no way I'm goin' down there!" Eugene screamed. John blew out a sigh of frustration.

"Did you hear that?" John asked Trip over the phone. For the past thirty minutes, the group had been discussing the best plan to find the bomb. After a bit, John thought it might be best to bring Trip into the talks. John had agreed to go below with Eugene, but Eugene was not having it.

"Tell him I'll get his sentence reduced," Trip said, thinking Eugene was holding out for a deal.

"He's going to get your sentence reduced," John said to Eugene.

"Nope, still not going to do it," Eugene said, shaking his head.

"Let me have five minutes, and I'll get him to show us," Jessica muttered.

"What did Agent Hammerstein say?" Trip asked. John shot a look at Jessica. Jessica threatened John with a look if he told what had happened between her and Eugene earlier.

"Jessica thinks that Eugene is sweet on her, and she can get him to change his tune," John said to Trip. "I'll call you back once we know something." John quickly hung up. Jessica was giving him a withering look.

"I thought you had trouble lying?" Jessica said.

"It's not a lie," John replied. "You think every man walking has some humongous crush on you." Jessica stared daggers into John, and John ignored her. After a second she turned toward Eugene.

"Let me tell you something, Eugene. If we don't find that bomb, my career could be over, and if my career is over, I'm going to sit in the backseat with you all the way home and let John drive. I'll be extremely upset. Do you wish to ride with me beside you in the backseat for all those hours?" Jessica asked, her voice quiet and calm. Eugene turned to John.

"So, if I tell you where the bomb is, you'll get my sentence lowered?" Eugene asked, almost pleading. John nodded with a slight smile on his face.

"It takes a big man to admit when he's wrong, and do the right thing Eugene," John said.

"I don't think you understand," Eugene replied. "I'd rather die in a bomb blast than ride back with that woman sitting beside me all the way home."

"You know that means I have to ride beside her on the way home," John replied. Jessica gave John another dirty look.

"You have a gun," Eugene replied. Chet burst into laughter. Jessica whipped around and gave him a dirty look for good measure.

"I'm not sure that's enough," John said, leading Eugene to the doorway.

Chapter 65

"Wait!" a voice called out from the group as John and the team started down the stairs. John turned and saw AJ starting toward them.

"If anyone is going down there, I'm going with you," AJ said. "Before you start arguing with me, I know this compound better than anyone. If something goes wrong down there, I am the best chance you have of getting out of there." John, Jessica, and Chet all exchanged looks. Chet finally nodded in agreement.

"He's got a point, John," Jessica said, begrudgingly.

"I don't like it, but we don't have many options at this point," John admitted. "First time you think something's not right down there, give the word and we all get out, understand?" AJ nodded.

"I'm no hero," AJ admitted. John still didn't move towards the stairs. "I promise, John." John relented and led Eugene toward the stairwell.

Eugene led them down the hallway and took a turn just before they got back to where John had found AJ and the rest of his group trapped. After several twists and turns, John was sure he had no idea how to get out of the structure. Finally, Eugene stopped just before they got to doorway.

"That's it," Eugene said. "Inside, there is a locker with the bomb."

"That's where Brad kept things for class," AJ said quietly.

"Brad Smith?" Jessica asked. AJ nodded.

"Is this the same guy who locked all of you in the cafeteria area?" John asked. AJ nodded again, very sadly. John started inspecting the door, moving in front of the group.

"Something has led him off the path of light," AJ said quietly. John didn't know about all that, but what he

166

did know was if this guy made bombs, there was nothing stopping him from booby-trapping the room, door, or some random object inside. Not able to find anything, John turned back toward the group.

"AJ, how many bombs has Brad made?" John asked.

"I don't know," AJ admitted. "He told me he had turned his back on that life." John watched AJ very closely. There was something there, but it wasn't a lie. Jessica nodded to Chet to take AJ down the hall. She led John a few steps away.

"Did your spidey-sense get anything?" she asked.

"Spidey-sense?" John asked.

"Well, what do you call it?" Jessica asked. John thought for a second. "We really don't have time for this. Can you tell anything?"

"There's something there, but he didn't lie," John said. "It could be simply that AJ thought Brad had changed, and AJ found out he hadn't." Jessica nodded and led John back to AJ.

"Are there any bombs in that room that you know of?" Jessica asked, point blank. AJ shook his head no; Jessica looked at John.

"He's telling the truth," John said. "But, the problem is there may be bombs he doesn't know about."

"I'm aware of that," Jessica snapped.

"Come on now, no reason to explode," Chet said, looking at his two companions with a big smile on his face. "No reason to explode," Chet said again.

"Really?" Jessica asked. "Really? We could be blown to kingdom come, and you think this is a good time to be tossing around puns." John looked a little irritated.

"He's trying to lighten the mood, Jessica," John said, defending his friend. "What are you doing?

Chastising him for trying to get you to stop worrying? Well, how dare he." AJ stepped in between the two.

"Perhaps we might all admit we're a little stressed, and just let it all go," AJ said. John and Jessica exchanged a look and gave a begrudging nod. John headed for the door where the bomb was supposed to be.

"Why don't you make her go first?" Eugene offered. John looked over at Jessica.

"You've got a fan," John said, grinning. Jessica nodded toward the door impatiently. John opened it, and realized he had been holding his breath while doing so. They all filed into the room. No one said anything as Eugene pointed toward a locker. John walked over and opened it. They all crowded around and looked in. They weren't sure whether to be glad or not. The locker was empty.

Chapter 66

John and Jessica had gone back outside to call Trip to apprise him of the situation. Jessica made the phone call, while John tried to think of what to do next. John stood outside the bunker, looking over the property trying to visualize where the bunker was laid out underground. He didn't hear anyone come up behind him, and he was a little startled by the voice.

"Pretty country here," Jessica said. John whipped around, saw it was Jessica, and relaxed. "Sorry, I didn't mean to startle you."

"It's this case," John replied. "It's got us all a little on edge. We're all doing things I don't think we'd normally do." Jessica looked at John, trying to decide if that was a shot or a way of him saying everything was okay. She decided to play nice and believe he was trying to bury the hatchet.

"Do you understand how someone would want to live like this?" she asked, trying to change the subject. John nodded.

"Away from others, off the grid, a charismatic leader telling you that you were doing things the right way as an assurance...sure, I get it," John replied, looking back over the countryside.

"Do you think he's that charismatic?" Jessica asked.

"No, and that's why he has a small cult which does seem to be harmless, unless you've found something?" John asked. Jessica shook her head.

"No, I think they're absolutely harmless, they just apparently have some followers that are a little out there. When I talked to the group earlier, I couldn't find anything to worry me or make me think they were doing anything wrong. It looks like one former member just lost it," Jessica replied. The charismatic leader comment kept playing through her mind, and she couldn't let it go. "So,

169

you think if their leader was more charismatic that there would be more people here?" John was still looking over the landscape.

"Absolutely," he replied. "It's a good thing I'm not egotistical enough to have ever decided to start my own cult."

"If you did, we would probably have to hunt you down with all the charisma you possess," Jessica said, almost laughing. John was still looking away and didn't see her face.

"See, you get it," John said, not realizing Jessica was making fun of him. "Sam always thinks I'm too full of myself, but there are people out there that admire me and want to follow me."

"It must be hard being you," Jessica said, her face red from not laughing. John, oblivious as usual, just plugged right along.

"Thank you for noticing," John said sincerely. "Too many people don't take the time to think about all I have done and how hard it is. I mean I can talk to anyone and tell they are lying. People think I have some spiritual gift, and they want to learn from me, or be like me, or follow me. Do you know how hard that is sometimes?"

"How do you do it?" Jessica said, just barely stopping a laugh at the end of her sentence.

"It's just hard work," John said. "And humility." With that, the floodgates opened, and Jessica laughed like she had never laughed before. It took John a second to realize what was going on. He turned around, trying to fight the embarrassment that was washing over him. "I'm so glad for your honesty."

"I figured you'd just use your superpowers to see through it," Jessica said through bouts of laughter. "You have to be careful, John. The enemy could abduct you and use your powers for evil!" Jessica began to laugh again.

She laughed so hard that she went down to one knee. John just shook his head and started back into the bunker. Jessica tried to say something to him but couldn't through the laughter. John passed Chet on the stairs and just kept going. Chet came outside to find Jessica trying to compose herself from laughing so hard. Chet just looked at her, confused.

"He told me that he thought he would make a great cult leader," Jessica said, still snickering. Chet just nodded.

"I'm just glad he doesn't use his powers for evil," Chet said, to which Jessica burst back into laughter.

"You're not helping!" John yelled from the base of the stairs. Chet and Jessica ignored him.

Chapter 67

John went back downstairs and tried to find AJ. After about five minutes of getting lost, John found the stairs and headed back up. Chet and Jessica were still having a good laugh at John's expense.

"Miss us?" Jessica said, clearly enjoying herself.

"Not really," John replied. "However, I can't find AJ, and I need to talk to him."

"I'll show you where he is, boss," Chet offered. John started back down the stairs and then stopped. He came back up with an evil grin on his face.

"Why don't you go talk to the children and make sure there's nothing going on, Agent Hammerstein?" John offered.

"I really think you could use me to interview AJ," Jessica replied. John shook his head, the grin growing. He was going to enjoy this.

"It's more of a conversation and not an interrogation," John replied. "Besides, I'm sure we all can agree we don't want to subject children to me any more than they already have been. Chet here is prone to say something that will do nothing but get himself into trouble." John was having trouble fighting the smile on his face, and he could see Jessica was starting to steam. John pressed on. "No, Jessica, it seems you're the only one of us that should be interviewing children." With that, John turned and headed down the stairs, proud of himself.

"I really hate you," Jessica said in a low voice.

"I heard that," John replied from down the stairway. John waited for Chet to join him at the bottom of the stairs.

"Was that really necessary, boss?" Chet asked.

"Probably not," John admitted. "But, I just couldn't take anymore of her. Let's talk about something more pleasant. Like did you find out anything about the mysterious Brad Smith?"

172

"Sure did," Chet replied. "Apparently, our Mr. Smith bombed a factory where his wife died a few years back. He said that the factory had unsafe working conditions. There was an investigation after Mr. Smith's wife died, and nothing was found to substantiate his claim. He bombed the plant shortly thereafter and was thought to have died in the explosion, but apparently, that was incorrect."

"Is the bomb we found in New York similar to the one used at the factory bombing?" John asked.

"The techs are working on it," Chet replied. "But, so far, there's nothing to show that the signatures are different."

"How many died in the explosion at the plant?" John asked.

"That's just it, boss. The bomb went off in the middle of the night. It completely destroyed the plant, but the only one thought dead was Mr. Smith," Chet replied. "He was identified by his dental records, so there is the possibility that the whole thing was faked. His dentist did admit there was a break-in shortly before the time of the explosion, but he thought nothing of it at the time since nothing seemed to be missing."

"So, we have an ex-bomber who found some type of religion and decided to go clean, and now, he's out making bombs again," John summarized. Chet nodded. "The question is who, or what, made this guy start building bombs again?" Chet shrugged.

"No idea on that one, boss," Chet answered.

"Does Brad have any family?" John asked. Chet shook his head no. "So, with his faked death, there would be no one to identify the body. That was nicely played. Is there anything that suggests he had training in explosives?" Chet shook his head no.

"Boss, it appears he learned it all on the internet," Chet admitted.

"That's why I don't want any part of it," John replied. Chet sighed. His and John's fight over all things electronic was legendary in the office "I'm telling you, it won't be long until everyone gets bored of it."

"You cannot be serious!" Chet exclaimed. John nodded.

"I mean, what's next? Getting online and spouting off your opinions and pictures of what you're going to eat that day?" John asked.

"Well that would never happen. That's just ridiculous," Chet replied.

"I agree, it's ridiculous," John replied. "I'm telling you, it's just a matter of time. Oh, don't forget pictures of pets. They'll be everywhere." Chet just shook his head at the ridiculousness of John's claims. They came to the office where AJ was. The leader of the group was going through a file. "I've never seen a preacher, or whatever you call yourself, take notes on his members."

"Brad was the only one I ever took notes on," AJ replied.

"You'll excuse me, AJ, but that seems awfully suspicious," John said. AJ nodded.

"It's because I always wondered if Brad truly repented," AJ admitted. "I feel bad for doing this, but I feared this day might come, and I didn't want any blood on my hands or on the church's."

"That's all well and good," John began. "But, at the end of the day, you knowingly harbored a fugitive--not just a fugitive, but a man that can and has created and deployed a bomb. Brother AJ, each person that dies is on your head." AJ hung his head.

"I know, Agent Fowler. I know."

Chapter 68

"Why don't you start at the beginning," John offered. AJ nodded.

"I met Brad a few days after he blew up the plant that he blamed for killing his wife," AJ said. "I know that it was proven there was no wrong doing by those that owned the plant, but I'm telling you, Agent Fowler, there was a lot of money that changed hands for the ruling to go the way it did."

"I wouldn't be surprised," John answered. "But, you do realize, regardless of the plant's guilt or innocence, blowing up a place is wrong?" AJ nodded.

"That was the center of many of my and Brad's conversations," AJ replied. "We discussed his actions of saving countless future lives by destroying the plant. We talked about him needing to repent for his actions. Brad and I had talked for several days, and it always came back to the same thing. The discussions went back and forth about how he had done no harm to anyone, but he had broken a law. The argument was centered around that it was man's law, and all he had done was retaliated in the vein of an eye for an eye. I became concerned for what he might do. I didn't have the conviction that he deserved to go to jail, but I was afraid what might happen if he were left alone."

"So, you're telling me you took him in to keep an eye on him?" John asked. AJ nodded sadly.

"Obviously, something changed him," AJ said. "Over the past few months, he seemed more aggitated and began, I believe, to think he could get the attention of the world for things they had done wrong. He began talking about how so many believed more in things of this world than of the next life. He constantly complained how the college football team had this huge stadium that was filled every Saturday they played and on Sunday, no matter what a person's religion was, they couldn't be bothered to attend their place of worship. Something wasn't right with him, and I meant to keep a close eye on him, when we had some other problems within the community." John was staring at AJ.

"Care to elaborate?" John asked. AJ looked a little uncomfortable.

"You have to understand. I think everyone is a part of God's children," AJ began. He paused and looked at John.

"Just tell me, AJ," John said. "All I want is to catch Brad and his bomb." AJ nodded.

"In the past, we have taken in many people that may not have been born here," AJ offered. He was waiting for a reaction from John.

"So, you have housed those who are considered illegal aliens?" John asked. AJ nodded reluctantly.

"We had a group of people who did not have proper documentation, but all they wanted to do was worship in their own way, raise their family, and be happy. Is that asking too much?" AJ asked, his eyes pleading.

"I don't mean to be harsh, AJ, but I have got to find a bomb, not have a political debate about the rights and wrongs of illegal aliens," John answered. "What does this have to do with Brad Smith? And, why were all of you locked up in the cafeteria when we got here?"

"There were several families here that were subject to deportation, and someone had tipped off the authorities that they were here," AJ answered. "We were being watched, and I couldn't let them be sent back. So, I spent the past several weeks devising a plan to get them out of here. During that time, I didn't pay any attention to Brad. It was during this time, I later found out, that Brad started working on a manifesto. He had his first and second graders write it in class." John and Chet exchanged a glance, AJ paused. "You've seen it?" John nodded.

"It took us a bit to figure it out, but you just confirmed what we thought," John answered.

"It's my fault," AJ admitted. "I did tell him I would like him to work with the children on their writing. I left it up to him as to what they needed to write. I never tell anyone exactly what they need to do, Agent Fowler. All I can do is lead people." John had been studying AJ. Something kept nipping at him occasionally. AJ wasn't lying, but something wasn't 100% spot on. John wrote it off to AJ trying to protect his people and not sharing everything. Besides, he wasn't here about the cult. He was there about finding a bomb.

"One night, we told the illegals that we had an escape plan mapped out," AJ said softly. "We loaded them onto a truck, and they were taken away. I don't know where, because if I don't know, I couldn't tell the authorities if they ever asked. It was right after the truck left that Brad locked us all in the cafeteria and took the bomb he had made."

"Any idea where?" John asked.

"He said he was going somewhere that everyone would know about the explosion," AJ answered. John studied AJ. What AJ said was the truth, but there was something else. John just couldn't quite figure out what.

"AJ, listen," John began. "If there is anything at all, please tell us." AJ paused.

"He did say that he would do away with the false prophet worshipping," AJ said quietly. John looked at Chet in confusion. Chet shrugged. It was at that moment that there was a knock on the door. The two turned, and there was Jessica who waved them into the hall. The two men headed into the hall, leaving AJ by himself. AJ turned back to his desk as a slow smile covered his face.

Chapter 69

"There have been other people here that have disappeared," Jessica said quietly. John nodded and told Jessica what AJ had told them about the illegal aliens. Jessica sighed, bummed that she hadn't cracked the case.

"There's something he's covering up, but it's something tiny," John said. "It could be something as simple as something he thinks he's doing wrong. Honestly, everyone gives off some kind of guilt cues at some time."

"Are you sure, boss?" Chet asked. "Are you sure it's nothing?" John thought for a second and nodded.

"It's something tiny," John reiterated. "He's probably holding something back to protect something within his church, or following, or whatever it is."

"How do you know that?" Jessica asked.

"His body doesn't give off any tells when it comes to Brad," John replied. John paused and thought for a second.

"Are you absolutely sure?" Jessica asked.

"No," John admitted. "I'm not 100% sure how this works, and I have been wrong before, but I'm pretty sure we're not going to find Brad here. He's going somewhere to stop false prophet worshiping." Jessica nodded, and the three started to walk back toward the entrance.

"Sounds like he's going to that football stadium he talked about earlier," Chet said offhand. John and Jessica stopped mid-stride and looked at each other, horror on their face.

"What!?" John exclaimed. "What did you just say?" Chet was trying to think what he said wrong.

"Well, he was talking about how the local college football team fills the stadium every Saturday," Chet began.

"That stadium holds over 100,000 people," Jessica said softly. She was almost in shock. The color had drained from her face. John felt sick to his stomach.

178

"It would make a statement," John said, looking at Jessica. "Today's Saturday, isn't it?" Jessica nodded. "What time?" Jessica looked at her watch.

"The game starts in less than three hours," she said, almost in a whisper. John broke into a run down the hall.

"Call Trip, and get them to begin evacuating that stadium!" he yelled. He ran into AJ's office, startling him. "The football stadium in Knoxville--could the bomb be there?" AJ gulped and nodded.

"Yes, yes it could," AJ answered, and with that, John was gone. He raced up the stairs. When he exited into the sunlight, he was nearly blinded. Jessica was already in the car, yelling into the phone at someone. Chet and Eugene were both in the back seat, neither one looked very happy about being there. John ran, opened the car door, hopped in, and the car sped off toward Knoxville and the football stadium. AJ came up out of the bunker as the car sped away. His followers all turned to look at him.

"I believe we have work to do," AJ said, and the group slowly began to go back in the bunker. AJ watched the car speed away in the distance. He pulled out a cell phone and made a phone call. He waited for the person on the other end to pick up. "They are on their way to the stadium," he said into the phone. AJ listened to the voice on the other end and smiled. "I gave my answers as vaguely as I could. I think a couple of times he thought something but wrote it off." AJ listened for a minute and nodded. "Of course, we'll begin recruiting the new followers immediately." AJ disconnected and headed inside, whistling tunelessly.

Brad Smith
8 Years Ago

Chapter 70

Brad was surprised how easy it was to get past stadium security. He examined the drawing in front of him one last time to make sure he had put the bomb in the correct place. Satisfied that he had followed his instructions to the letter, he began to tear apart the drawing and eat each piece. When he had gotten rid of all the evidence, he found a dark place he could observe his work and wait. He began to think back to the day he had met Brother AJ, and his whole life had changed.

It had all started a few days after the bombing. Brad had wanted the company to pay for what had happened to his wife and had planned everything out perfectly. He had found dental records of a cadaver, broke into his dentist's office to switch them out, and then made sure that the body was close enough to the blast to be almost impossible to be identified. He had the perfect plan except for his conscience.

It was a couple of days after the bomb exploded that he first thought about turning himself in. He was sitting in a small diner, contemplating going to the local authorities. It was the right thing to do. He had made his statement, and it was time for people to know about the evils that corporations were hiding just for the sake of the almighty dollar. His wife had died, and the authorities and those in justice had done nothing but cover up her death. People needed to know why he went to the lengths he had, and that couldn't happen if everyone thought he was dead.

Brad had nearly summoned all the courage he needed to turn himself in when the diner door opened, and

Brad first met the man who had changed his life. Brad had never seen Brother AJ until that moment. He wondered if God had smiled on him that day by that chance meeting. For days, Brad had thought someone was watching him, almost surveying him. At first, he had thought it was the police or even someone from the factory that had been hired to keep tabs on him, but today, he knew. It was God. It had to be. How else would Brother AJ have known that Brad was at his weakest in that exact moment?

The first thing Brother AJ told him was he should not turn himself in. Brad smiled and chuckled over the thought now. It had been the constant talks with Brother AJ that had convinced him he was doing God's work. God had told him to blow up that plant. The owners of the plant were more concerned with money and things of this earth than they were of people's overall well-being, both physically and spiritually. It had taken several visits for Brad to see that, but with the help of AJ, he knew that he had been given a new gift from God. He was now God's messenger.

Brad had never felt as loved and as needed as he had when AJ brought him to his new home, The Temple of Light and Hope. Brad didn't understand at first what they were doing until AJ explained things to him. So many people of this once great nation were deaf and blind to God's teachings, it would take a new tactic to bring people back to the church, more specifically, AJ's church.

One of the ideas AJ had was finding those who were not legally in the country. The church would feed and clothe the immigrants. They would teach them the church's way and then take them to new lands where they could do the work they were told to do, spreading the gospel by their deeds. Brad was sure some outsiders would see what they were doing as brainwashing, but what they were doing was saving the immigrants' souls and, hopefully, soon saving the souls of their new masters. Brad thought the method was a good one, but it would take a long time to get any type of results--results they might not see in their lifetime, much less the people whose souls they were trying to save. He was talking to AJ one night when he brought up that very point. That was the day Brad's position in the church changed forever.

Chapter 71

"Do you really mean that, Brad?" Brother AJ asked. Brad gave AJ a confused look. "Do you really think we should speed up our plan? Not out of lack of belief in God, but because these people aren't ready to believe because they only see that which is right in front of them? The people of today are a people of instant gratification. They can't understand something that doesn't reward them immediately, and we both know that our faith's reward is not something that happens immediately. We're told in His word that our time on this earth is full of trials and tribulations, aren't we Brad?" Brad nodded. "Do you think we need to speed things up?"

"I would never go against God and his teachings," Brad began carefully.

"But?" AJ asked. Brad swallowed, uncomfortable.

"But, many people are going to die and not receive their blessings because they didn't believe," Brad answered, fearing reprimand.

"What you say is something some would call blasphemy," AJ answered. Brad nodded. "I wouldn't, but some would," AJ added to Brad's surprise. AJ smiled at his follower's astonishment.

"Come now, Brad, have you ever known me to admonish someone for their thoughts when I counsel them on a one on one basis?" AJ asked. Brad shook his head. "Are you interested in helping those who are lost find the Lord?" Brad nodded, curiosity bubbling up inside of him. "Are you willing to make the ultimate sacrifice, Brad? Are you willing to die? Are you willing to go to jail while protecting the church? Are you willing to be mocked and made fun of?" Brad nodded vigorously.

"You know I am!" Brad exclaimed. "I want others to be able to feel the freedom and joy that has come over me since you helped me see the light!" AJ nodded and smiled.

"What I propose is dangerous, and you might die," AJ said quietly.

"Anything!" Brad exclaimed. AJ smiled.

"I prayed and prayed I might one day find the perfect person to help me one day spread the word," AJ said. "What I need is for us to never speak of this project, and if asked, I will have to deny that I approved this." Brad smiled.

"What do I need to do?" Brad asked. AJ shrugged. He got up and walked around his office until he came to a poster of the football stadium in Knoxville. He stood by it where Brad couldn't help but see it.

"After the terror attacks in New York, many came to find their lives were void of God," AJ said.

"You want me to attack someone?" Brad asked. AJ shook his head.

"I would never condone something like that," AJ said. "The loss of life that day was terrible, but think how much worse it would have been if they had understood our culture enough to know not to attack our jobs, but our places of escape." AJ looked up at the poster. When he looked back at Brad, there was a smile on Brad's face.

"I think it best if you had plausible deniability," Brad said. AJ looked confused.

"Deniability of what?" AJ asked. Brad just smiled. AJ walked over to a file drawer and pulled out a notebook that he handed to Brad. "I think the children need to practice writing this week from oral dictation." Brad thumbed through the manuscript and smiled. "You know one other thing that could have been devastating to the country? If our people in law enforcement had known about this happening and not been able to stop it. Just think how awful it would be if someone in New York were to discover such an insidious plot and not be able to do anything to stop something horrible from happening, again."

"Are there two members that I could use for an errand?" Brad asked innocently. "There are some things I need delivered up north that I can't be seen doing." AJ smiled and nodded. Brad reached out and shook AJ's hand. "Thank you for this opportunity to repay you for all your kindness."

"Thank you, Brad, for being of the church and not of this world," AJ responded.

Chapter 72

Brad opened his eyes. He took a second to get readjusted to his current surroundings. He had gotten lost in his thoughts. He gathered himself and stared at where the bomb was hidden in the darkness. There were 11 more "mini" bombs hidden around the structure. They were all controlled by the main controls on the bomb Brad was staring at. Between the 100,000 or more people in the stadium, plus all of those in the parking lot just tailgating, Brad was sure he would achieve maximum collateral damage. He heard a walkie talkie static break the silence. He listened very closely. It was obvious something was going on. He looked down at his watch. The bomb was set to go off in a little over two hours. Brad had worried about this part of the plan. He didn't want the bomb going off too soon and not maximizing its payload. He built a timer on the bomb instead of a remote detonator. The "mini" bombs were all set up where if the main bomb didn't go off, they wouldn't go off either. It would be an epic explosion, one that would surely get a nation's attention.

Brad heard the walkie talkie again; it was closer now. He slipped deeper into the shadows. A guard walked by, never seeing Brad or the bomb. He didn't look very concerned.

"All clear down here," the guard said into his walkie talkie and walked off. Brad shook his head in disgust. The security guard couldn't even be counted on to do his job properly. Brad had no idea what the guard thought a bomb would look like, but there wasn't going to be flashing lights on an arrow that read "bomb" pointing toward it. Brad wondered if he wasn't doing the human race a favor by getting rid of some of the people that were going to die today.

Brad looked at his watch again as it slowly counted down to the upcoming kickoff. He hated this waiting game and the unnecessary loss of life by the people attending this game, but their loss was part of the greater good. Brad felt at peace knowing how many people would turn from their wicked ways with this act. Brad smiled in the darkness at the flashing red light that was barely visible on the bomb across the way. It wouldn't be long now.

John and Jessica
Now

Chapter 73

John and Jessica walked down the street hand in hand. John thought for a second he was probably a little too old to be acting like a newlywed, but he looked over at Jessica and pushed the thoughts from his mind. Over the past three years, he had gotten used to being alone. Honestly, he had been alone for most of his life. The way he thought about things, the way he reacted to the knowledge, and especially the way he trusted his instincts had made many around him feel like John was bored being around them. For John, there was little excitement in everyday life. He knew almost everything going on before anyone else did. Mysteries became his obsession. Not just mysteries, but puzzles. John could get lost in a case and not think about anything else as easily as the normal person could enjoy a lazy, rainy Sunday afternoon. What John didn't have the past three years was someone to keep him grounded in the real world.

John never understood how Sam dealt with him. He knew there were times she wanted to strangle him. When Sam died, the part that bothered John the most was the thought in the back of his head that he was going to be alone for the rest of his life. That thought angered him. How dare he think about himself with his wife being dead? John wondered what Jessica would say if she knew she was the person John thought about most in those three years after Sam's death. Granted, many of those thoughts were absolute anger with what had happened in the interrogation room after Sam's death but not all of them. John smiled at the memory of him picking up his cell phone one night three different times just to call Jessica, not having any idea what he might say.

John glanced over and saw Jessica watching him.

"Wanna share?" Jessica asked.

"Just thinking about how lucky I am," John answered. The smile that crossed Jessica's face was indescribable.

"Please don't ruin it by saying something you would normally say," Jessica said softly.

"What do you mean?" John asked, confused.

"You can say things that you mean as one thing, and a person can take as another. But, instead of taking it as a win, you have to go explain your meaning and ruin a moment," Jessica explained. John didn't think he was ever going to understand people.

"So, you'd rather believe what you wanted to hear instead of what I was actually trying to say?" John asked. Jessica shrugged.

"Sometimes," she answered.

"So, I shouldn't tell you that I was thinking how lucky I was that there is someone else in this world that understands me besides Sam?" John asked. Jessica sighed.

"You didn't ruin it as bad as I thought you would," she answered, shaking her head. John started to ask her what that meant when a car backfired, startling everyone. John jumped and reached for his gun by habit. He chuckled when he realized what had actually happened. He turned toward Jessica and started to speak when he saw her face. The concern wasn't that she thought it was a gun shot, it was something else.

"Are you okay?" Jessica asked, trying to feel his pulse. John pulled his hand away.

"I'm fine," he answered. "What's wrong with you?" Jessica didn't answer, concern written all over her face. John put two and two together. He closed his eyes for a second to gather himself. He opened them and spoke. "You thought I was about to have an attack? You thought the backfire was going to make me think about the attack by Bruce again?" Jessica didn't answer, but she didn't have to. Her face told the story. John sighed and looked around. They were a few feet from the front of an ice cream shop. John took Jessica's hand and led her inside.

Chapter 74

Jessica prepared herself for one of John's rants, but he didn't. Instead, he walked over to the self-serve flavors of ice cream. Jessica was a little confused.

"John," she began.

"They have cheesecake flavor," John said.

"John, you have to," Jessica began, but it registered what he said. "That's just wrong."

"And over there you can get graham cracker crust, fruit, or even candy to put on top of it," John said, pointing toward the bar that contained multiple toppings.

"Seriously, why would you put anything on cheesecake?" she asked, deadly serious.

"I wouldn't do the fruit, but some hot fudge and those little bars of toffee and chocolate," John trailed off. He looked at Jessica, and he swore a little drool was coming down the side of her mouth. They both made their ice cream cups, paid for them, and found a seat. Neither said a word for a few minutes as they enjoyed their dessert. John looked at Jessica; it seemed she was in heaven.

"This was an excellent idea, Mr. Fowler," Jessica said with a smile on her face. "I never would have thought of this." Jessica studied him for a second. "I guess we should talk about this."

"Talk about what?" John asked, his famous grin at the corners of his mouth.

"I will hurt you," Jessica said, seriously.

"I'm recovering from a gunshot wound," John replied.

"I know," Jessica responded somberly. John sighed and put his ice cream down. He took Jessica's hands and looked her in the eyes.

"What's going to happen the first time someone shoots at me?" John asked.

"I'm going to worry that you're having an attack," Jessica replied honestly. John nodded.

"That's what I'm afraid of," John said. Jessica looked at him confused. "If you get hurt while being worried about me, I'll never forgive myself." Jessica pulled back and sat back in her seat, pulling her hands from John's. She thought about what John said. She had never given it a moment's thought before.

"I guess that is something I'm going to have to work on," Jessica said.

"Would it make you feel better if I promise you that if I start to have another attack I will tell you immediately?" John asked.

"Are you sure you can, or will you freeze up again?" Jessica asked. John pursed his lips and sat back in the booth. He hadn't thought about that. Jessica crossed her arms in front of her, a satisfied smile growing out of the corners of her mouth. John shook his head and chuckled.

"You just enjoy any chance you get to get the better of me, don't you?" he asked. Jessica leaned across the table and took his hands again.

"John, we both know I learned from a master," she said, to which John touched his chest and tried to look surprised. Jessica smiled and went on. "Besides, the majority of our relationship has been somewhat confrontational and combative." John had to agree.

"I guess you're going to blame that on me?" he asked. Jessica smiled.

"I'm just as much to blame as you," she replied softly. "Now, I promise to try and keep my head when it comes to any gunshots I hear and how it may affect you, but I can't promise I won't jump now and then."

"I guess that's all I can ask," John responded. The two sat there for a second, staring at each other. John glanced to the side for a moment and saw a couple of

192

teenagers that were watching them. He looked back at Jessica with a huge grin. "Want to gross a couple of teenagers out?" Jessica shook her head.

"No," she answered, dropped John's hands, and began to get up from the booth.

"Who's the old one of the couple now?" John asked, getting out of the booth. Jessica had turned around to throw away their trash. When she heard John's dig, she got a determined look on her face, spun around, put her trash back on the table, grabbed John and kissed him in front of everyone. The teenagers made a gagging noise.

"Get a room," one of them said. Jessica released John. He looked over at them out of breath.

"Not a bad idea," he answered with a grin on his face. Jessica hit him in the shoulder, but not as hard as usual. He looked at her, and she was trying to look at him disapprovingly, but he saw through her act. They threw away their trash and headed out into the New York night.

Knoxville, Tennessee
8 Years Ago

Chapter 75

Jessica pulled up to the stadium, her mouth opened in shock. No one had left the stadium. In fact, people were continuing to file in. She uttered something that John didn't quite make out, but if it was what he thought she said, he had thought something very similar. She pulled up to the entrance where a man at a gate was letting people in. He looked at them and sighed.

"Now, look here, little lady," the security guard began. Chet snorted. If John hadn't been so upset by the stadium not being evacuated, he would have enjoyed this, but they didn't have time. Jessica reached into her pocket and pulled out her credentials while putting the car in park. She grabbed the door handle, whipped it opened and jumped out before the guard had a chance to say anything else.

"F. B. I," she said with a growl. The guard visibly and audibly gulped. "Why hasn't this stadium been evacuated?" The guard didn't know quite what to say. "Never mind, get me the person in charge. Not your boss, the person in charge!" The security guard fled, while Chet got on the phone with Trip. Chet told Trip what was going on. It sounded like Trip was going nuclear on the other end. Jessica was blessing someone out over the phone. A cart pulled up, and a man, who trying to look very official while looking flustered, got out.

"What is going on here?" he asked. John thought immediately that he didn't want the answer they had for him.

"We're trying to stop over 100,000 people from dying," John said like he was having a normal conversation. "What are you doing?" All color drained from the man's face.

"We had our guards search the facility, and they didn't find anything," the pompous official retorted, sweat pouring down his face. Jessica and John exchanged looks. John wondered what it meant that they were both thinking the same thing. He decided now wasn't the time to care. Jessica asked the question they were both thinking.

"Exactly what were you looking for?" Jessica asked.

"Well, a bomb, of course," the official replied. Jessica just stared at him, waiting for him to continue, but that was all the official had to say.

"And, what does a bomb look like?" she asked. The official began to look very uncomfortable. Jessica was seething. "Start evacuating that stadium now!"

"Now, see here, little lady," the official began. John grabbed the official and pushed him against the car, spread-eagle. "What are you doing?" he sputtered. Jessica looked surprised.

"One, I'm arresting you for hindering our investigation," John replied. "Two, I'm probably saving your life for calling her "little lady." Three, I'm going to arrest everyone here until someone starts evacuating all these people."

"Okay, okay! I'll start evacuating!" the official exclaimed. John turned to Jessica. Jessica looked amused.

"Are you asking me if it's okay to let him go?" Jessica asked. John nodded. "Normally, I would say just let him sit and stew awhile, but we are kind of pressed on time." John let the official go. He made some calls over the walkie talkie, and people slowly seemed to be leaving. John looked around. There were thousands of people in the

195

parking lot, that were in no condition to drive and had no intention of driving that day.

"We'll never get these people out of here in time," John said, disgusted and impressed at the same time of the brilliance of the plan.

"We've got to find that bomb," Jessica said to him softly. John turned to look at the stadium. They would have to go in there and try to find it before it went off. John turned back toward Jessica.

"At least, we'd go out with a bang," John said with a grin. Jessica rolled her eyes and groaned. She got into the car, wondering if she got out of this alive if she really wanted to continue working with John.

Chapter 76

John, Jessica, Chet, Eugene, and several stadium officials gathered in an office, looking at the designs of the stadium. John watched Eugene. Eugene seemed oblivious to what was going on. He walked over to him.

"Where would you put the bomb, Eugene?" John asked. Eugene shrugged.

"I've got no idea," Eugene said. John studied him. He wasn't lying, which confused John.

"Eugene, do you know anything about bombs?" John asked. Eugene grinned and shook his head. John groaned. They had been wrong. They had been so sure that Eugene and Bubba Ray were vital to the plan.

"Decoys?" he asked, already knowing the answer. Eugene didn't answer but smiled. Jessica looked at John, confused.

"Do you have somewhere we can stash him, locked up, away from the stadium?" John asked one of the officials. The official nodded and made a call into his walkie talkie. A second later, a security officer entered the room.

"I need you to lock him up away from the stadium," John said to the officer. The officer nodded. "Make sure he doesn't get away because if this thing goes off, he is to be charged with conspiracy to commit murder for each person that dies or is injured."

"Hey!" Eugene yelled as he was being led away. "Wait!!" John motioned for the officer to stop. "I didn't do any of this, but one bomb isn't going to bring this whole place down." John turned and looked at the plans of the stadium. "For maximum effect, you'd want a lot of explosions simultaneously."

"Where's the main supports?" John asked. One of the stadium officials started to point toward spots when John stopped him. "Let's say you were going to demolish

197

the stadium for some reason, where would you put the charges?" The official went white. He got a pen and started circling spots on the diagram. When he finished, there were twelve spots circled. The official looked ready to pass out. "What's wrong?" John asked, knowing this was more than pressure.

"I had a student the other day studying architecture ask me the exact same question," the official replied. Jessica muttered something under her breath. John felt his heart sink.

"He said something about slave units," Eugene said.

"So, there's a main charge?" John asked. Eugene nodded. John turned back to the diagram. "Of those twelve spots, which is the most out of the way? Which one could someone put something and it wouldn't be seen?" The official thought for a second and pointed.

"There's some stuff stored there that's very flammable as well," the official said.

"This guy's batting a thousand," John muttered. "Okay, you get eleven teams, and check out these other spots. You're probably looking for something small. He wants enough to blow the supports. The main blast is probably here," John said, pointing to the spot just circled by the official. "That's where my team is heading." John signaled for the officer to take Eugene away.

"You'll have to kill him!" Eugene yelled.

"Wait!" John yelled to the officer. "Why do you say that?"

"Because he's willing to die for what he believes in," Eugene said. John nodded for the officer to take Eugene away. John turned back toward Chet and Jessica.

"These things never end well," Chet said quietly. John was praying his friend was wrong.

Chapter 77

John, Jessica, and Chet headed toward the section of the map that the official had told them he thought would be the best place to hide a bomb. Chet was talking back and forth on a walkie talkie. The other teams had begun to report in small devices in the other eleven areas the stadium official had circled on the map.

"Chet," John whispered. "You need to turn that thing off."

"I'm going on radio silence," Chet said into the walkie talkie. Jessica looked over at John who was shaking his head. She couldn't help but laugh.

"Cut him some slack," Jessica said. "He doesn't get out much."

"I just hope he doesn't shoot the bomb," John replied. Jessica would have thought that was hilarious if it wasn't a possibility of happening. They neared the spot that the official had told them about. In the darkness, John swore he saw a faint red glow. He pointed it out to Jessica who nodded. John crept toward the glow when he felt something come out of the darkness and hit him in the legs. The two scrapped for a few minutes until John found a blade at his throat.

"Drop it! FBI!" Jessica yelled, gun pointed at the man holding a blade to John's neck. The man pushed the blade a little closer to John, and Jessica dropped her gun, and from the shadows, another gun came sliding down the concrete.

"I mean, really, Chet? He didn't even see you!" John yelled. The man pressed the blade against his neck again, and John was quiet.

"Brad, you don't want to do this," Jessica said. Brad looked surprised for a moment and then gave her a nod.

"What do I not want to do?" Brad asked.

200

"Well, besides blowing up this stadium, you don't want to hurt him," Jessica said. "That guy you have a knife to has no one that cares about him but his wife." John looked at Jessica in shock. "I mean if you killed him, there are people at the bureau that would throw you a party."

"I see," Brad said. "What are you doing?"

"Me, I'm getting an even bigger star on my folder," Jessica said. John's mind was racing. What was she doing? "Here's the deal. You have a much bigger bargaining chip if it was me you had hostage."

"Let's say you're right. How would I manage?" Brad asked, intrigued.

"Switch the knife to your left hand and put it at John's throat. Take your right hand. Get his gun," Jessica said pointing to John's gun. Brad followed the instructions. "Now, point the gun at me," Jessica said. Brad followed the instructions. "Now, let go of John," Brad hesitated, then let John go. John looked at Jessica and back at Brad. "John, move, don't be a hero," John did as he was told. "Now I'm going to walk over, and you have me as a hostage." Brad put his left arm around Jessica's neck and the muzzle to Jessica's head. John was shaking his head when he caught Jessica's eyes. Oh, boy. This was going to be bad. Jessica winked at John, and then, all he saw were blurs.

Jessica shot her right hand up, hitting Brad's right hand and pointing the gun harmlessly into the air. At the same time, she shifted her weight and flipped Brad over her back. The gun went flying, and Jessica grabbed Brad's left arm as he flew by. Brad hit the ground, and Jessica put an arm bar on Brad. Brad was screaming. John turned to Chet.

"Should we help him?" John asked. Chet shook his head.

"A lot of these nuts believe in suffering," Chet replied. "I would hate to interfere with his religious freedoms." John slipped his hands in his pockets and nodded in agreement. Chet went to retrieve their weapons. Jessica finally let go of the arm bar and went to Chet to get her gun. Brad was on the ground, groaning. Jessica pulled her weapon out and pointed it at Brad.

"Get up, Brad!" Jessica yelled. "Playtime's over, and it's about to get real."

"Can she say that?" John asked Chet.

"Are you going to tell her not to?" Chet replied. John thought, nodded, and turned to Jessica.

"I guess it's time to get real," John said to Jessica, a twinkle in his eye.

Chapter 78

"This is what's going to happen," Jessica said as she cocked the trigger on her weapon. Her gun was trained on Brad. "We're going to go over to that bomb and start cutting wires." Brad's smile grew as Jessica spoke. Jessica had an evil grin on her face, knowing what Brad was thinking. "What you don't know is I've got a human lie detector machine over here that will tell me when we've hit the wrong wire. So, if you think you're going to get to blow me up, you've got another thing coming." Chet leaned over to John.

"I didn't know you could do that," Chet whispered. John gave him a quick look. Chet gulped. "You can you do that, right?"

"I don't know," John replied, starting to get a little worried. "I've never tried anything like this before." Jessica still had her gun trained on Brad and was continuing her speech.

"Besides, you're probably not even at the front of the line of people wanting to blow me up," Jessica said, glancing at Chet. Chet smiled. "Chet, you can sit this one out if you want. There's no sense in all of us dying in case John's wrong."

"Can I sit this one out?" John asked, hating the whole plan the more he thought about it.

"No, I'm with you guys," Chet said, ignoring John.

"Thanks, Chet," Jessica said. "I guess I was wrong about you." Chet beamed. John still wasn't thrilled with the plan.

"I don't like this idea," John said, desperately trying to think of anything else they might try instead of cutting bomb wires while he watched Brad's reaction.

"Nobody asked you," Jessica replied, not taking her eyes off Brad. "You could just tell us which wire, Brad.

You don't want to go up in a cloud of smoke, if I'm wrong about this, do you?"

"If I die, then I go out doing my mission and spreading the word to the sinners and those who are caught up in this world and not in the next one," Brad replied.

"I don't want to go out," John said to anyone who would listen to him.

"What kind of man are you?" Brad asked, disgusted by John and his perceived cowardice. "These two are willing to lay down their lives to their cause. I don't agree with their cause, but I respect their honor."

"Honor gets you nothing if you're dead," John replied, getting frustrated from being stuck in the middle of Jessica's plan. "What is it with people and this dying with honor crap? Dead is dead. I agree, I would rather die saving someone's life than getting shot in some senseless shootout, but to die for honor or whatever it is, is just stupid."

"Do you believe in God?" Brad asked.

"I do, but I don't for a minute think God told you to do this," John answered.

"That is for me to know," Brad answered sagely. John threw his hands up.

"How about this, bucko," John countered. "I don't believe in what you do. If you want to kill yourself, I guess at the end of the day, that's your business, but you don't have the right to take me with you. What you're doing is terroristic. What you are doing is killing people just to kill people and scare them. You're not changing anyone's mind about his or her beliefs. All you're doing is trying to frighten people to follow your religion. What is it that makes you better than me that you can tell me who, what, or how I worship, or express my faith? What gives you the right to do these things?" John was furious. He didn't realize how furious he was until he began talking, and by

204

the time he was done, he realized he was nearly in a rage. Brad just smiled.

"You aren't worthy enough to understand my God," Brad replied. John thought he might explode.

"If you choose to believe in a vengeful God, then that's your choice, but you don't have the right to kill all these people because of your beliefs!" John yelled. Jessica had a strange look on her face. If John didn't know better, it was almost admiration. It was like she didn't know he had depth or layers to him. John pushed those thoughts from his mind. This wasn't the place, and who knew in this hyper-sensitive situation, what thoughts were going through anyone's mind.

"John," Jessica began. "I can't do this without you." John groaned and thought for a minute. He didn't know if this would work, but if he didn't try, thousands upon thousands would die. He finally relented.

"If I die, I'm going to haunt you," John replied.

"I'll be dead too," Jessica offered.

"I don't care. I'll still haunt you," John said obstinately. Jessica shook her head, and in spite of the situation, she found a smile was forming on the corners of her mouth. She decided now was as good a time as any to try out her plan.

"Let's get a move on," Jessica said. Jessica flicked her gun at Brad, and he started to where he had the bomb planted. Chet followed, while John just stood there for a minute, racking his brain for a last second way to get out of this mess. Chet turned toward his friend who had a sour look on his face.

"You can do this," Chet said.

"You're placing a lot of faith in me," John answered.

"That's why you're our fearless leader," Chet replied.

"Would you like to be in charge?" John offered. Chet just stared at John. John threw his hands up in disgust and started after them. "I don't know why everyone is in such a hurry."

"Because the bomb is on a timer?" Chet offered. John had forgotten that. John began to jog after Jessica, passing Chet. "Where are you going?"

"To disarm a bomb before it blows us up while we're discussing how much I'm against being blown up," John replied. Chet shrugged and took off after him.

Chapter 79

The four of them gathered around the bomb. Chet held a gun on Brad. John was in a position where he could see both the bomb and Brad at the same time, and Jessica knelt in front on the bomb, gently fingering the four wires. John was more than a little nervous.

"Should you be so close?" he asked Jessica. Jessica turned toward John with an amused look on her face.

"You do know that if this goes off, as close as I am, I'll never feel a thing?" she asked. John thought for a second. Should he move closer? Jessica shook her head, still amused, and pulled out a pair of clippers. She looked at all the wires and tried to figure out where to start.

"Do you know if you have to cut them in a certain order?" John asked. Jessica stopped, turned toward John, and gave him a look.

"I have exactly as much bomb training as you do," she replied. John glanced over at Brad. He was enjoying something.

"Is there a timer on there?" John asked, watching Brad. Brad turned toward John and smiled. Jessica started looking, and a gasp escaped her lips.

"We've got less than five minutes," Jessica said. She put her clippers up to the black wire, and bile shot into John's mouth. He didn't know when the last time he had been this frightened. John shook his head to try and gain control of himself and remembered he was here to watch Brad. John wasn't sure what it was, but Brad didn't want Jessica to cut that wire.

"Wait," John said, still watching Brad. John didn't understand what he was seeing. Brad seemed to be happy. So, was Brad happy that he wasn't going to die, or happy because that wire would have disabled the bomb? John wasn't sure. "We've got a problem."

"You mean other than four minutes?" Jessica asked. John swallowed. This was more than a bit of a pressure cooker.

"He doesn't want you to cut that wire," John said. Surprise filled Brad's face. Glee covered Chet's. John continued. "I just don't know why." Chet looked as though he could cry.

"John, if we don't do something, we're going to die," Jessica said simply. John studied Brad. Brad was obviously enjoying this. John made a decision.

"Cut the wire," John said. Jessica snipped the wire. The look on Brad's face told John what he needed to know. Nothing blew up, and everyone, except Brad, gave a sigh of relief.

"Great job, Boss!" Chet exclaimed. "How did you know?"

"I didn't," John replied. Chet repeated what John said slowly and then turned white and fell to the floor. Jessica looked at John, unsure of what to do. John pulled his gun and aimed it at Brad. Jessica smiled at John.

"Guess it's up to us," she said. She paused and then added. "Partner."

Chapter 80

"So if we live through this, what are you going to do this weekend?" John asked Jessica, gun still trained on Brad. Jessica turned toward John, confusion covering her face.

"Are you asking me out?" she asked.

"No! I was just trying to lighten the mood and talk about something other than our imminent death!" John replied. "Shouldn't you be cutting?" Jessica spun back around and glanced at the timer.

"Three minutes," she said. John had to decide what was next, green, red or yellow. Jessica was moving the clippers around, and John couldn't get a read on Brad.

"Yellow," John said. Brad looked at John, surprised. Jessica moved the clippers to the wire and held them there. Brad stared defiantly at John. "Try the red one," John said. Jessica moved the clippers, and John couldn't get anything off of Brad. "Try the green," John offered. Jessica moved the clippers, and John knew immediately. "NO!" he bellowed. Jessica stopped.

"Okay," she said, not moving a muscle. "We've got to do something." John was confused with what he saw . . . unless. "Take the gun." Jessica gave John a strange look and took the gun out of his hand. John took the clippers and examined the wires. He opened the clippers and placed them around the yellow wire. He glanced up at Brad and saw the same expression as before. John smiled, pulled the green wire down until both the green and yellow wires were in the clippers' cutting path. The look on Brad's face told him all he needed to know. He cut the wires.

"Gottcha," John said. He watched Brad and noticed two things, defeat and a growing hope on Brad's face. Why was there growing hope? He turned toward Jessica and saw sheer terror on her face. She was looking at the bomb. John followed her gaze. The timer had doubled its countdown! At that moment, Brad lunged forward taking down Jessica and her gun. The two of them bumped John, sending his clippers flying across the room. John looked at the bomb. He could never get to the clippers, get back, and cut the wire before the bomb exploded. John did the only thing he could think of. He reached in, grabbed the black wire and pulled as hard as he could. As he felt the wire tear away, he closed his eyes and braced for a possible explosion, which didn't come. What he wasn't ready for was the gunshot he heard.

Chapter 81

John opened his eyes and looked up. Chet had recovered his gun and fired a shot over the struggling Brad and Jessica. Brad relaxed and held up his hands. John thought he saw Jessica throw a punch, but he was wrong. She threw an elbow into Brad's face. Brad's eyes rolled back in his head as he fell off her, unconscious. John also noticed Brad appeared to have a broken nose. This was through no great powers of observation; there was just a lot of blood pouring out of it.

"Someone might want to plug that," John said, still not trusting himself to move. Chet holstered his gun, found some rags, and tried to plug the bleed the best he could. Chet got on the walkie talkie given to him by the stadium officials and began to radio for help. Jessica got up, went to find her gun, and came back over to John. She offered him a hand to get off the ground. John gladly accepted it, not trusting his trembling legs at that moment.

"Anything on the other bombs?" John asked Chet. Chet held up a finger; he was listening to the chatter coming over the walkie talkie.

"Sounds like all the bombs have gone from a red light showing on them to a green one," Chet replied. John exhaled and looked over at Jessica. Jessica had a satisfied grin on her face.

"This is what we call a win, right?" she asked, obviously proud of them. John couldn't help himself. His own grin began to grow.

"Yep," he replied. "You can see that I was right." Jessica looked confused. "Earlier, I told you how people always look up to me and want to follow me, and it's things like this that just go to prove my point."

"You can't be serious?" Jessica asked, truly believing John was joking.

211

"Of course I'm serious," John replied. "You would have killed us if it wasn't for me."

"Now wait just a minute," Jessica began. While this was going on, people had arrived to attend to Brad's injuries. Chet made sure that Brad was secure, looked over at John and Jessica arguing, shook his head, and called Trip. Jessica and John had no idea this was going on around them. Jessica continued. "You guessed on some of that."

"Sometimes my best guess is better than 99% certainty from most agents," John replied, trying to look as modest as possible while saying that. Jessica put her hands on her hips.

"I admit, you have some abilities the rest of us wish we had," Jessica said. "But it was my idea to try this tactic. If it was up to you, we'd still be looking for the bomb, and you would be whining about getting blown up."

"I did not whine," John said.

"I think you just need to admit we make a pretty good team," Jessica said, ignoring his comment. John paused, disarmed. He nodded.

"You're right. We do, and I'll gladly let you on as my partner," John said, reaching out his hand. Jessica smiled.

"I know I'm right, and that's why you can be my partner," she said reaching out her hand for John to shake. John looked down at their hands, both extended but not touching, then back at Jessica.

"Just as long as you know I'm lead agent," John said. Jessica shook her head.

"Un-uh," Jessica said. "I'm the lead agent."

"Will you two knock it off!" they heard Trip yell. They both looked around to see Chet on his cell phone, it was on speaker. "Agent Fowler is the lead agent since he is the senior agent."

"Well, he is older," Jessica said quietly. John shot her a look. Trip continued like nothing had happened, but John swore he heard a bit of laughter in his voice.

"Job well done, you three," Trip said. The three all exchanged looks, shocked. "Come on home." Chet started to end the call, thinking it was over when Trip came back on the line. "And, don't kill each other," he added, exasperated.

Chapter 82

The next day, the three gathered in Trip's office to hand in the final report on the case. Trip looked it over, glancing up at each agent at different times. When he finished, he leaned back in his chair and looked at the other three.

"And that's how it all happened?" Trip asked. Chet squirmed a little in his seat. John had included certain versions of the truth at different points to cover up any infighting between the three. Chet wasn't really comfortable with the account, but he had been down this road before with John.

"More or less, sir," John answered. Trip looked at Chet. Chet nodded quickly. Trip looked over at Jessica who nodded as well.

"Sounds good to me," Trip said, sitting back up in his seat and signing off on the report. The three agents exchanged looks. John started to stand.

"Well, if that's that, it was a pleasure working with you two and, of course you, Trip," John said, standing and straightening his coat. "I've got those cold cases I wanted to look over." Trip nodded and waited until John had turned and took the first step for the door before he spoke.

"I assume you'll be attending the New Year's Eve gala hosted by the senator?" Trip asked. John stopped midstride. He closed his eyes and groaned internally. He put on his best smile, opened his eyes, and turned back toward Trip. As he turned, he noticed the look on Jessica's face. There was sorrow on it. Surely, she wasn't sad that this was over? Surely, she didn't want this train wreck of a partnership to continue?

"Of course I'll be there, Trip," John replied. "Nothing short of a direct order from you to have to work on some case would keep me away from there. You don't

214

have anything you need me to do that night, do you?" Trip smiled.

"Oh, no, John," Trip answered. "That might get me on your wife's bad side." Trip's finger traced absently over the file in front of him. "I think the senator will get his funding on his team. Whoever that team is will have special clearance and backing from both the FBI and Homeland Security. That team would pretty much pick their own cases since they would have the authority to look at anything."

Trip paused for a minute to let what he was saying sink in. Chet glanced at John. John saw the look on his friend's face.

"Are you sure that's a good idea, sir?" John asked. Trip's head slowly rolled back and forth on his shoulders while he thought about it.

"I don't know," Trip answered honestly. "I mean with the right personnel on the team, it might be. The team wouldn't have to worry about political red tape. However, they would have to report to me, but there would be very little I could actually make them do. If the right three people were to run this team, they might be able to infiltrate the mob, organized crime, terrorists, or track down leads that most of us think are just too thin. It would be perfect for someone who loves puzzles, who has computer skills, and who is an unbelievable interrogator. But, of course, that one person doesn't exist."

"Why?" Jessica asked. "Why would anyone want to put that team together?" Trip smiled.

"Some people believe there is a great deal of corruption in this country, and the only way it's going to be found is through transparency," Trip answered. "When FBI agents answer to a few select people, then they can be steered in certain directions. The way this new taskforce is set up, this team has priority over any case. I could suggest some cases, but the team could always say no." Jessica glanced at John. John's face was unreadable. "Anyway, I won't keep you three. Enjoy Thanksgiving on Thursday." John stood there a minute as Jessica and Chet got up to leave.

"You said it won't be announced until New Year's Eve," John said. Trip nodded. "What do we do until then?" Trip smiled.

"I guess you three could work together or on your own. Your call," Trip said. John nodded and walked out the door, past Jessica and Chet.

Chapter 83

John headed to his desk, picked up a file, and started looking through it. His mind wasn't really on this case. Since the three of them had started working together, some other agents had been moved and now he, Jessica, and Chet were all working and sitting together. John sometimes thought they all ought to move downstairs to the foxhole, but that was for newbies. John ran a hand through his hair. He was out of this team-up mess as long as he could convince Sam it would be best.

"Do you hate me that much?" the quiet voice came from behind him. John spun and saw Jessica there with Chet, standing right behind her.

"What do you mean?" John asked.

"You heard what he said. We could be THE team in the FBI," Jessica said, anger running across her face. "And, we can't because of you. Why is that John? Why can't we?"

"Look," John began. "Chet is going to be head of IT one day. You're going to be the director of the FBI and tell me what to do on an everyday basis, but me?" John shook his head. "I can't do this team-up stuff. This buddy-buddy cop movie thing we're doing doesn't fly with me. Jessica, I'll only slow you guys down. I can't handle red tape and all that stuff."

"There won't be any red tape!" Jessica exclaimed. "Did you listen to Trip?" Around the corner, Trip had left his office and trailed behind them. He listened to the conversation out of sight. This had been the biggest worry. For all of this to work, John had to want the team, and right now, he didn't.

"Do you really believe that?" John asked. "Don't you realize the fact this is being approved in DC is proof enough it's full of red tap?"

"Do you want Bruce to get this?" Chet asked. John's head shot up like he had been slapped. "You know he'll get this if you don't take it, and if he wants us on the team..." Chet trailed off, shaking his head.

"That will never happen," John said. "Jeremiah will kill the whole thing before Bruce gets it."

"And, if he doesn't?" Jessica asked. Before John could answer, another agent approached the three.

"I don't mean to interrupt," the agent began. "But Agent Hammerstein, we could use your help with a suspect. We have him in interrogation, but we can't break him."

"She can do it," John said. Chet and Jessica looked at him in surprise. "What?" he asked. Chet and Jessica exchanged a look between them. "I'm not heartless." John turned to the agent. "If anyone can crack your suspect, it's her."

"Thank you," Jessica said softly. Chet shook his head. The agent turned to Chet.

"Agent Morris, if it's not too much trouble, could you take a look at this?" the agent asked, producing a hard drive. Chet was torn.

"Go do your thing, Chet," John said, patting the closest thing he had to a friend on the back. "You, too," he said to Jessica. Jessica and Chet exchanged glances. John saw on their face it was over. He hated to do it, but it had to be done. The three separated, and John was glad for the peace and quiet as he began to dig into his newest cold case.

Trip watched the three part. He had one card left to play before he gave up on this. He went to his office and called Sam.

Chapter 84

When John got home that night, he fixed his wife his world famous pizza, that is if world famous meant him and his wife. Sam came in the door, saw the dinner, and knew what John was up to. She would have regardless if Trip had called her or not. Trip and Sam had talked for quite a while, and they had a plan to put into motion. She wasn't sure John would appreciate it, but it was for his own good.

"Hey, sweetie," Sam said as she went through the living room.

"Just in time," John answered. "Dinner is ready."

"Great," Sam answered. "Trip called me earlier." John stopped dead in his tracks. This was unexpected.

"Sam, before you start," John began. Sam held her hand up and shook her head. John stopped talking. When Sam got the look on her face she currently had, there was no fighting her. John prepared for trench warfare.

"Trip thinks the three of you are incompatible," Sam said as she walked toward the table. She sat down, leaving John standing there, his jaw dropped. "Are you going to join me?" John walked over to the table, in a bit of shock.

"So, you're not going to push this?" John asked.

"Why?" Sam asked as she took a bite. "Oh! You have out done yourself this time, John." John was completely disarmed. He wasn't sure what was going on. Sam continued. "You did what I asked and gave it a try. That's all anyone can ask. The only person I feel sorry for is Jeremiah. This program is going to go through, and he's scrambling to make sure Bruce doesn't get it." John's head snapped up. He looked at Sam carefully. She was telling the truth.

"He can't," John said. "They can't give it to Bruce. They just can't."

219

"Well, it's not your problem, sweetie," Sam answered taking another bite. "You didn't like it. It didn't work, and it's not like you guys teaming together again would be easy on you. I mean, it's obvious. You work best alone. Sure, Chet gives you a leg up with his computer knowledge. Jessica is a great interrogator, and when push comes to shove, she's got your back. I mean, I thought you all were becoming a great little family, admittedly a dysfunctional family, but a family all the same. I mean, you have to do what's best for you." John didn't know what to say. "Let's be honest. It would never work."

"But, we did save lives," John admitted quietly. Sam shrugged.

"Who's to say what would happen next time?" Sam replied. "The three of you just can't coexist. No one can force the three of you together. It's over, John. Now, eat your dinner, or I'll eat your part," she said with a smile on her face. John found he wasn't that hungry. He couldn't get the words he had uttered out of his head. "But we did save lives," played over and over in his head. Sam fought the smile that threatened to cover her entire face as she enjoyed her dinner, and John thought.

Chapter 85

Thanksgiving passed, and December seemed to roll right along. There weren't a lot of big cases and very few that really needed John's abilities. John dug through cold cases, trying to find new leads. He filed reports on the cases and was beginning to become frustrated from not hearing anything back. Chet continued to work in the cyber unit, and Jessica was using her skills to break suspects when needed. Chet and Jessica were flourishing, but every time John saw them, they didn't look happy.

"What's bugging you, Chet?" John asked one day shortly before Christmas.

"I don't know, John," Chet replied. John gave him a look, and Chet sighed. "I miss what we did."

"What do you mean?" John asked.

"I mean I was part of something, now...now I'm only a cog in this large machine," Chet replied.

"That's crazy," John said, not believing what he was hearing. "You are the best there is at what you do."

"Yeah, but when it was us, we got to do what we wanted," Chet replied. "Now, I'm being led around and told what to do and when; the thought that we could work any case...it just hurts." John didn't know what to say. Chet mumbled something about getting back to work and hurried away. John saw Jessica in the hallway and thought about talking to her. As he started toward her, another agent told her she was needed. Jessica sighed and followed after the agent. John wondered if she was feeling the same way as Chet. They were being used by those higher up to advance their careers. John hated it, but it wasn't his problem. What was his problem was him not hearing back on his cold cases. He decided it was time to talk to Trip. John headed to Trip's office. The door was open. Trip saw him and waved him in.

"I've been meaning to tell you good work on those cases, John," Trip said. John looked confused.

"So you have been reading my reports?" John asked. Trip turned around and handed him all the paperwork that John had sent through the past few weeks. All the leads had panned out, but the cases had been worked by other agents.

"Why wasn't I brought onto these cases?" John asked, confused. Trip was a little surprised.

"Why would you?" Trip asked. "You don't work well with others and enjoy your space. I'm letting you do what your best at."

"Just like you're letting Chet and Jessica do what they're best at?" John asked, starting to get angry. Trip nodded.

"I'm just using the tools that I have available to me," Trip answered, a little smugly.

"So we're being punished," John said, not asked. Trip shook his head.

"No, I'm the person in charge and I decide who does what around here," Trip answered. "I mean pretty soon there will be a team that I won't be able to tell what to do, but until that time, I'm the boss. Now, why don't you use some of that vacation time you have built up? How about I not see you back at work until the day after the New Year's Eve ball?" John stood up, straightened his coat, turned to leave, and then lost it. He spun, slammed his right hand flat on Trip's desk, and with his left hand, pointed at Trip.

"The three of us don't work well together! Your games aren't going to change my mind! If you won't use me to the best of my ability, then maybe I'll just go over your head!" John exclaimed. Trip's expression never changed.

"I agree with you. The three of you are a disaster waiting to happen," Trip responded. "And, as for going over my head, who are you going to go to? The one friend you have, you've put in a terrible position. Who's going to go to bat for you? You've made your decision; now live with it." John was seething, but Trip was right. John turned to leave. Trip smiled and quickly dropped it before getting in one last jab. "I guess I lied," Trip added. John spun, never seeing the smile on Trip's face. "As of January 1, the new team will be named. I guess you still have time to change your mind." John stared daggers into Trip and then walked out. He had a decision to make, but not the one Trip thought. John had to decide if he wanted to remain with the FBI.

Chapter 86

A man sat alone in a dark restaurant. He was dressed in a very expensive suit. He was sitting by himself with a few men seated some ways away. The men were keeping an eye on him, and there was the unmistakable bulge of weapons under their jackets. The man was enjoying a slice of pizza when the front door opened. He looked up at the familiar figure that walked in. The newcomer walked up to him.

"Mr. Brown, I presume," the man that entered the restaurant said. "Call me Mr. White." Mr. Brown grimaced.

"Do we really need to do this?" he asked Mr. White. Mr. White shrugged.

"If they're listening in, then they'll never know who's talking," Mr. White answered. The "they" he was referring to was the FBI.

"What's this about?" Mr. Brown asked. Mr. White arranged his coat, looked at the long-time made man, and decided to be straightforward.

"It's about Duck," Mr. White said. Mr. Brown closed his eyes, hoping this wasn't going where he thought it was. Mr. Brown opened his eyes and nodded for Mr. White to continue. "We need to take care of the problem."

"Duck?" Mr. Brown asked. Typically when made men talked about a problem, it meant for someone to get whacked. Mr. White nodded. Mr. Brown stood and motioned for Mr. White to do the same. "Let's take a walk." Mr. White nodded; he had figured that would happen. Typically when one wanted to discuss business, the two would take a walk, so they couldn't be heard on surveillance. Mr. Brown's men began to follow, but Mr. Brown slightly shook his head no. The guards sat back down, still on high alert. The two men headed outside.

"While he's not Boss of Bosses, Duck is the closest thing we've had in years," Mr. White said. Mr. Brown nodded. Duck took the lead in the meetings when the families gathered together. He had cleaned out all of the rats some years back and was still well respected because of that. "While his first plan was original, many of his associates are bringing too many eyes on us." Mr. Brown had to agree. All of Duck's non-Italian friends were causing the FBI to take a hard look at them. The FBI always seemed to have it in for the families, but with all of the extra activities by Duck's friends, there were more eyes on them than ever, and that made doing business hard. This was especially true since that babbo, Bruce, tried to whack John Fowler. In fact, it was by Duck's order that John was never to be whacked to begin with. Between that order and that Fowler was FBI, John was basically untouchable. Whacking a FBI agent was just asking for trouble they didn't need.

"He can't be broken," Mr. White went on. Mr. Brown had to agree with that. Sometimes, a member could be knocked down or demoted in rank; that was what Mr. White meant by broken, but it wasn't possible with the position Duck was in. Mr. Brown couldn't believe how open he found himself to this idea of a hit on Duck.

"What does this have to do with me?" Mr. Brown asked. Mr. White paused and then continued.

"Obviously this can't be an on the record hit since Duck is on the Commission, but it's also not that off the record. You're the final vote. If you vote no, Duck gets a pass. If you vote yes, then most feel you should assume the throne and be the boss. The boss of all," Mr. White added very quietly so that no one could overhear.

Mr. Brown was stunned. Basically, he had just been told it was his call if Duck lived or died. If Duck died, it would be by the board's approval. Of course, this was all to be done without Duck's knowledge. If this hit happened, then Mr. Brown would be promoted to the what the media called Capo di Tutti Capi, Boss of Bosses. Mr. Brown swallowed.

"What about his own little private Commission?" Mr. Brown spat. The thought of this Commission made most made men sick. Duck had created his own little group that contained non-made men. It was despicable, and Duck deserved to die just for that.

"Without Duck, they have nothing," Mr. White said. "Archibald is smart enough to know not to cross us. Everyone feels he would just walk away. He doesn't know enough to ever hurt us. We feel that if he doesn't come after us, then there is no reason to go after him. As for the other one, he tends to do whatever Archibald tells him to." Mr. Brown nodded as he continued to walk. "This is a huge decision, and no one expects you to make it today, tomorrow, or even next week. There were certain people that wanted you to know that if you wanted to make a change of leadership, I can get a place ready." Mr. Brown nodded. Mr. White had just told him that he would find a place to bury the body if it happened.

"Don't we want it public?" Mr. Brown asked, scarcely believing the words coming out of his mouth. Mr. White smiled.

"I've got a guy I could vouch for to do it public," Mr. White said. "I just ask if the books open, he gets a fair opportunity." Mr. White was telling Mr. Brown that he had someone he trusted with his life, that was willing to do the job, if the hit man could become a made member.

"Let me think about this," Mr. Brown said. Mr. White nodded and headed to his car. Mr. Brown stood outside alone, wondering if it was a time for a change.

Archibald Staples, Prison
Now

Chapter 87

Archibald walked through the prison slowly. The guard that had been assigned to Archibald watched him carefully. Archibald wasn't on suicide watch, officially, but he did currently have one guard that was assigned to him at all times since his breakdown. The warden had his eyes on the prize. If he could get Archibald to admit all he did, the warden knew he had a great political future ahead of him, and he wasn't about to lose Archibald now, not when he was close to breaking.

Archibald had been wandering all over the prison, even to some parts that had been closed down. This was nothing new. Since Archibald's breakdown a few days ago, Archibald had wanted to walk and reflect. Pastor AJ had agreed to see Archibald. It was just going to be a few more days before the meeting could take place. Pastor AJ had told the warden that before they met, Archibald needed to reflect on his sins, hence the long walks of reflection for Archibald. It was during one of these reflection walks that the guard thought Archibald was going to lose it. They came to a series of cells, and Archibald's mood changed.

He had been melancholy for several days, but upon entering this particular cell block, Archibald looked almost moved to tears.

"What happened here?" Archibald asked the guard with tears in his eyes.

"What do you mean?" the guard asked.

"It's so sad here," Archibald replied, nearly sobbing.

"There was a murder here," the guard replied, wondering if he should tell Archibald the truth. Archibald looked absolutely shocked. He grabbed onto the guard's arm like he might fall at any moment.

"Take me there," Archibald pleaded at a whisper. The guard thought, decided it would be okay, and took him to the cell. When they entered, Archibald seemed to almost lose it. "Tell me," Archibald pleaded.

"This was the cell of an inmate named Brad Smith," the guard replied. Archibald nodded. "He bombed a factory several years back. He said that his wife died at a factory due to unsafe working conditions. It was later discovered his wife was pregnant. The poor guy went nuts and bombed the factory to get back at the owners and supposedly save those that were working there. It was thought Brad died in that explosion, but it was discovered by a couple of FBI agents that he survived and tried to set another bomb a few years later at a football game. The agents caught him, and he was sentenced here. Some mob guy stabbed Brad to death a few months later. Brad died saying he had been set up, but there was nothing to show that was the case."

Tears streamed openly down Archibald's face. The guard had no idea what was wrong.

"It was my fault," Archibald said quietly. The guard looked at Archibald, confused. "The plant he bombed, it was my plant," Archibald admitted. "If only I had listened to him and not had my lawyers tell me I was doing nothing wrong…if only," Archibald stopped midsentence and broke down sobbing. The guard tried to console Archibald but couldn't. He radioed in for help, and within minutes, the prison medical staff was there to attend to Archibald. The warden pulled the guard aside to find out what happened. After the guard told him the story, the warden went to his office to call Pastor AJ. It was time to bring him in. The warden was afraid if he didn't do something soon, he was going to lose his ticket out of the prison.

Chapter 88

John sat in his living room, flipping through channels. He couldn't find anything that he remotely wanted to see. Reality TV made his mind almost explode, especially since he could spot people telling constant lies, and most TV crime shows he could figure out in minutes. That was one of the reasons he loved watching most sports. He never knew what was going to happen. He knew what most players would try to do, but the final outcome was always in question. The only one he didn't like was the MMA stuff. It was just so violent. John saw so much violence every day that he didn't want to see it when he came home; unfortunately, Jessica just loved it. Jessica walked into the room, saw what he was doing, walked over, and took the remote away from him.

"Why'd you do that?" he asked.

"Because we both know there is nothing on TV that is going to make you happy," she replied. She walked over, opened a red package and put a DVD in the DVD player.

"The fight you missed?" John asked. Jessica turned around and smiled. John returned her smile. When she turned back to the DVD player, John silently groaned and dropped his head backwards into the cushions. Jessica heard his head and whipped around, expecting to catch John doing exactly what he was doing. Instead, John was leaned back on the couch, smiling. Jessica sat down beside him, concerned. If he was already figuring out how to not be caught, she was going to be at a serious disadvantage in their disagreements. She decided to be devious. She leaned into him, with her head on his shoulder, and ran her hand over his shirt.

"You know I was thinking we could not watch this and instead, retire to the bedroom," she began. John began to grin like an idiot. She continued. "But, you seemed so happy to see this fight that I think we'll just go ahead and watch it." John started to protest a couple of times but stopped. He was certain he had been setup but had no idea how to prove it. John noticed the screen and stared.

"Is that two women?" he asked. Jessica smiled and nodded.

"Do you not think that women can fight in mixed martial arts?" she asked. John missed the tone of her voice.

"I guess," John replied, not really caring. Not for anything sexist, he just didn't care anything about MMA and would just as soon not discuss it. Suddenly, Jessica had a hold of his arm and was trying to wrap her legs against his shoulder.

"What are you doing?" John screamed, half afraid for his life.

"I'm showing you a flying armbar," she said, still trying to get the hold on.

"I tap, give, cry uncle, whatever!!" he screamed again. Jessica let go, a disappointed look in her eye. John held his arm and wondered if he had married a crazy person. His cell phone rang, pushing the episode from his head. He reached over to the table beside the couch to get it. He listened for a second, signaled Jessica who nodded, and both of them carefully moved to the door. They shut it behind them, leaving the lights on.

Chapter 89

Amanda was at her normal spot in front of John's building, watching the window. She hadn't seen movement in some time, but that was normal. There was flickering, and she was sure that the two of them were watching TV. She shook her head in disgust. How he could have sullied her mother by marrying that tramp he was now shacked up with, Amanda couldn't understand. Amanda glanced again at the black car sitting a little ways away. She was almost positive that someone was in it, and she was starting to think whoever was inside was watching her. Her father had always told her to know when it was time to cut your losses and leave.

"Nice night we're having," came the male voice behind her. Amanda closed her eyes, upset with herself.

"So, you finally decided to acknowledge my existence," she said, spinning around and looking John in the eye. John couldn't help but involuntarily gasping. The resemblance was uncanny. She looked so much like Sam that it was all John could do not to take his hand and run it across her cheek. "See something you like, perv!?" she almost spat out. John shook his head sadly.

"First off, I didn't even know you existed for sure until right now," John began. "And, secondly, you look so much like your mother, it took me off guard. I apologize if I offended you."

Amanda was a little surprised at his brazen lies. He had known about her existence and chosen to ignore it. She knew that because her father had told her. John looked at her and smiled.

"What?" she asked.

"I've told you something that you don't believe or goes against something you believed," John replied.

"You don't know me or anything about me!" she said fiercely.

"I'm sorry, but you're wrong," John said gently. "I know things about you, things you probably don't even know. I don't know how similar you are to her, but I would imagine given how you look like her, there have to be many other similarities."

"Why did you lie?" she asked. She didn't like John. He had caught her off-guard, and she didn't like that. Her father had warned her about him.

"I didn't lie," John replied. "I only found out that your mother was pregnant a short while ago. Your grandparents were told that you died during childbirth. As far as I know, she thought you died."

"You lie!" she spat. John shook his head.

"Look at me, Amanda," John said gently. "Do I look like I'm lying?"

"How would I know? Do you think people can tell if someone's lying just by looking at them?" she asked. John chuckled. "What's so funny?"

"You really don't know anything about me, do you?" John asked. Amanda wasn't liking this conversation at all. She got an almost evil smile on her face. She stepped right up to John and whispered into his ear.

"I know one thing that you don't," she said confidently. "I'm going to kill you, and there isn't one thing you can do to stop it."

Chapter 90

Amanda pulled away with a satisfied smile on her face that she had scared him. She was surprised at what she saw. John's world famous smirk began to grow across his face. As Amanda saw it, her smile faded. Why, she didn't know, but there was something about that smirk that said she was wrong.

"No, you're not," John replied, shaking his head. He rocked back on his heels. "You may want to kill me, but you won't." Amanda was furious.

"I don't know how to make it any simpler, you ignorant fool! I will kill you if it's the last thing I do!" she exclaimed. John was smiling at her and shook his head.

"No, you won't," he replied. "You not only don't know me, but you don't even know yourself."

"You're wrong," she snapped back. "You don't know me or my father."

"You're right," John admitted. "I don't know anything about him. Why don't you tell me all about him? How about you start with his name?" Amanda laughed at John.

"All you need to know is my father is the greatest man to ever live," she said with a satisfied smirk on her face. John began to get his famous smirk back on his face, the one that used to drive Sam crazy. This was the second time Amanda had seen it in one day, and she didn't like it. John could tell the smirk that Sam hated had the same effect on her daughter. "What?" John just shook his head. He looked off into the distance, ignoring Amanda. The smirk fell from Amanda's face. John knew he was winning this little jousting match.

"You're the proof I needed to open up the grave," John said.

"What grave?" she asked, confused.

"The one that you are supposed to be buried in as a baby," John replied. "That is if you really are Sam's child," he said as an afterthought. Anger flashed across Amanda's face. John knew his little dig had worked.

"You don't know me!" she screamed. "You don't know anything about my life. You just pretended I'm dead, so you didn't have to deal with me. You hated that she loved him more than you! You hated him and did everything you could to destroy him! I'm going to kill you for what you did to him and how you poisoned my mother against me." John shook his head, sadly.

"Sam didn't know you were alive," he countered calmly. Amanda spit in his face and glared at him.

"There! You want to know if I'm really her daughter? Now, you can test me! Didn't see that one coming, did you genius!" she exclaimed and stormed off. John didn't move to follow her. In fact, he didn't move at all. Within thirty seconds, Ron was beside John, taking a sample of the spit Amanda had spat on him.

"Actually, he did see that one coming," Ron replied. John looked at Ron in surprise, and began to chuckle. Both men couldn't help but laugh out loud. Amanda didn't know it, but she just helped prove that former President Nichols was her father.

Archibald Staples
Prison

Chapter 91

Archibald was led through the prison into a private room. There was the pastor from a few days earlier, Adam Johnson, waiting for him. Archibald was uncuffed, and the guard stationed himself by the door.

"If you don't mind," Pastor Johnson began. "I'd like some privacy to talk to Mr. Staples. I know what he is believed to be, but Mr. Staples is here to repent and I have no fear of him." The guard didn't like it but radioed in to the warden. The warden told the guard to do as the pastor said, and the guard left the room. Both men listened for footsteps to fade away. Pastor Johnson put his finger to his lips and pulled a small device from his pocket and began to run it along all the walls, furniture, and anything in the room that could hold a listening device or camera. Adam turned toward Archibald after he finished and smiled.

"We're clean," Adam said. Archibald smiled and walked toward Adam, arms out, and clasped him in a bear hug. They patted each other on the back. The two men broke the embrace.

"AJ," Archibald said. "How are you, my friend?"

"Better than you it appears," AJ answered. "You were right about creating this second identity." Archibald nodded.

"When you shave all that hair off your face and head, you really look nothing like the infamous Allen Jones," Archibald replied. "Is that alias done for with the haircut and shave there?" AJ shook his head.

"A wig and fake beard is all I need," AJ replied, smiling. "The congregation believes I'm off to talk to the

Lord right now, to find out what direction He intends to lead us, and how I can be a better leader. The followers are waiting for my return with great anticipation. Do I need to hold up on my end for a while with your incarceration?" Archibald shook his head.

"No," Archibald replied. "Of all our cargo, your followers are the easiest to deal with. The undocumented illegals aren't that bad, but your followers . . ." Archibald snorted a laugh. "I don't know how you do it, but it's like leading sheep to slaughter. They think they're doing God's will by going to some foreign land and working for eighteen hours a day. I don't know what you're feeding these people, but it's amazing." AJ smiled.

"I'm just preaching obedience and the belief that by their work, they will one day lead their lost masters to the Lord," AJ replied. "Out of curiosity, did you know this was the same prison that Brother Brad was incarcerated?" Archibald shook his head, not because he didn't know, but because he couldn't believe AJ would think that little of him that he didn't know.

"Of course I did," Archibald answered with a smile. "I even sent flowers to his family when he was shanked here. I think it was something about a disagreement over a card game. You shouldn't ever try to cheat one of those mobsters in cards." AJ smiled. Archibald looked very pleased with himself. "I mean just because the man bombed one of my plants a few years ago is no reason to hold a grudge." AJ was surprised.

"I had no idea what your endgame was," AJ admitted. "I always wondered why the elaborate plan to bring Brad in. I always thought it was a little dangerous to bring the FBI's eyes to the church." Archibald continued to look pleased with himself. "Now that I know that, a lot of things make sense. That was the first factory where we had some of your 'special workers.' I guess his days of bombings over working conditions caught up with him." Something occurred to AJ. "That was the last time you used the workers in one of your plants. So, in one bold move, you paid back Brad for what he did, and you made it seem like I was just a harmless preacher by setting Brad up to be a fall guy. The FBI saw that nothing was going on there, and it was the work of just one man. Any complaints they got against me, there was already a record, so it would take something serious to get another team down there to investigate me." Archibald nodded. "It's always amazing what I learn each time I see you."

"Well, I'm glad you're here," Archibald said. "I've not heard from Kenneth in several days, and I'm beginning to think I might have to plan an escape." AJ shook his head.

"Then, I bring good news," AJ said, grinning. "I've talked to Kenneth and was asked to tell you it will be taken care of in the next 48 hours. If it doesn't happen, I'll get you out, the way we talked about. I can hide you underground at the compound if we need to until you find a way out of the country, but if Kenneth is telling the truth, then you'll walk out of here a free man." Archibald smiled and nodded.

"Kenneth will do what he can," Archibald said. "It's a lot to ask a man to kill his father, but if anyone will, it's Kenneth." AJ smiled. "You know I never told you how proud I am of you."

"Oh," AJ said.

"You threw all the suspicion of any wrong doings on a couple of extremists in your following. What the FBI and John Fowler never realized is how loyal Brad and those other two men that set the bombs at the football stadium and were found with bombs in New York were to you. Everyone now thinks that Allen Jones is nothing more than a slightly quirky man with a following of a few harmless people. My boy, I am proud of you," Archibald said in admiration.

"Thank you. Not to change the subject, but we need to cover our bases. In case we're asked, what did we discuss in our meeting?" AJ asked. Archibald got an evil look on his face.

"We discussed how losing one's child is almost more than one can bear," Archibald said. AJ got a horrified look on his face.

"Archibald, are you sure that's a good idea?" AJ asked.

"It's perfect," he replied. "I was so grief stricken that we really couldn't get anywhere because of the emotion I displayed." AJ smiled and pulled a bottle of drops from his pocket and handed it to Archibald.

"I guess you better get started then," AJ said. Archibald began to put the drops in his eyes. As the tears began to run down his face, he was truly happy that he had only days left before he was free to begin his vengeance on John Fowler.

Senator Cosby's New Year's Eve Party
8 Years Ago

Chapter 92

John stood near the entrance looking over the entire room of the New Year's Eve party. John did not want to be here. He had told Sam about the words he and Trip had, and Sam could only say he had something to think about. John didn't want to quit the FBI, but he didn't want to be attached to anyone either. He didn't know what to do, so he watched the people mingling. Couples were dancing together and having a grand time. John saw Sam with the senator and shook his head. There were rumors that they were actually father and daughter, but there was nothing he could do about squashing them. Honestly to see them together, John could see where people could see that. The rumors weren't that important anyway; the people that mattered knew the truth. It was then John felt, more than saw, a person approach him. John did all he could to ignore the man who had walked up to him, but at some point, everyone has to acknowledge their boss, even at social gatherings.

"Trip," John said with a nod.

"John," Trip replied. The two men stood there in absolute silence for a few minutes. For most, it would be uncomfortable, but for John, he found the silence much more comfortable than the alternative of talking to Trip. He almost groaned when Trip turned toward him.

"I guess we were wrong," Trip said with an air that said it wasn't him that was wrong, but John.

"We?" John asked. "I don't remember me and you saying there was something we agreed on that wouldn't work." Trip ignored him and continued.

"This team up did work," Trip said. John wanted to shut his eyes and make the bad man go away. Trip would ramble on and on about how for the good of the FBI, the three of them should stay together. John didn't really care about the good of the FBI. What he cared about was what was best for him solving cases. The three of them had saved lives, and whether he liked Jessica personally or not, they had saved thousands, if not tens of thousands, of lives. Part of him wanted the team to continue, but part of him just couldn't see himself working with Jessica every day.

Those thoughts took less than a second to work their way through John's head. He opened one eye with a squint to see if maybe Trip had left, or possibly, he had finally used a Jedi mind trick to make him go away. To John's chagrin, Trip was still there and was still rambling on. John wasn't in the mood to hear one of Trip's rambles and looked around for someone carrying a bomb, machine gun, or even some bad fish if it would get him out of this. He saw the next best thing.

"Uh, sir," John began, interrupting Trip. He pointed across the room. "Isn't that Thelma?" He turned toward Trip, but Trip was nowhere to be seen. John chuckled to himself.

"Proud of yourself?" came the female voice behind him.

"Always," John replied, never turning around. He could see her fuming in his mind with his response. John decided it was time to deal with her. He turned to face Jessica and found out he was wrong. Jessica wasn't fuming. If anything, she seemed a little sad. John was slightly surprised. She looked conflicted but spoke anyway.

"I can't believe I'm saying this, but thank you," she said, extending her hand. A little suspicious, John took it. Jessica gave John a grateful smile. "You've taught me a lot. I'm just sorry this has to end. I think we made a pretty good team." John shook her hand, thankful for it all to be over. He felt eyes boring into the back of his head and turned toward where he thought the look was coming from.

John saw Sam, still talking to the senator and drinking a glass of champagne while watching him. John wondered what kind of superpower she possessed to appear pleasant and chatty to the person she was with but leave no doubt that she was unhappy with him, all while standing all the way across the room from each other. It didn't take someone with John's skills to figure out what she wanted. John made the slightest "really?" face, but Sam just kept staring at him. John sighed, defeated. He turned back toward Jessica who had her eyebrow raised looking down at their hands. How long had they been shaking hands? John knew this could go bad, but he plowed ahead anyway.

Chapter 93

John let go of Jessica's hand. Jessica shook her head, half disgusted, and started to walk off.

"Jess," he said. She stopped and turned to face him.

"Only my friends call me that," she replied coolly.

"Jessica," John began, and Jessica nodded. "There are some things I need to say." The look on her face told John she was trying to find a way to get away. "I'm sorry. I can tell you'd rather be out mixing and mingling." Jessica smiled a grateful smile and began to walk away. John continued his voice low where only she could hear. "I'll just let you read about it in the amendment to the official report," he added. Jessica stopped midstride and turned back toward him. John found he suddenly had Jessica's complete and undivided attention.

"Look," Jessica began. "I messed up, and I apologized for it."

"Messed up? Messed up!" John exclaimed, flabbergasted. He saw his wife out of the corner of his eye, giving him the stinkeye. How did she do that? He gathered himself, shuffled slightly where he couldn't see Sam, and continued. "Yes, you made some mistakes, some very terrible." Somehow, Sam had made her way back into his line of sight again and was giving him a look. Seriously, was she a ninja? "Mistakes that could have ended your career." Sam's eyes were drilling into him from across the room. He wanted to yell, "What?" at Sam from across the room, but he held it together and continued. "A career that looks to be very bright and promising," John added. Jessica's eyes softened; she looked surprised and a little happy.

"Thank you," she said softly. John was once again surprised with her reaction. Was Sam right? Did she really just want his approval?

"I don't want to see you lose that career with some bad choices," John continued. He was playing through every scenario in his head, but he could think of nothing that would get the result his wife wanted but one; it wasn't the result that John wanted. John swore Sam had somehow planted something in his brain to make him give in to her on this one. John sucked it up and continued. "I've given it some thought. We saved lives. Most days you don't get to say that. Most days you try and catch the bad guy after they've done something wrong and bring them to justice. We got out in front of something that could have been disastrous and came out ahead because when we had to, we worked together as a team." John took a deep breath and continued. "And, if you would like to continue on with Chet and me, then I say we keep the team together." In his mind he was certain he would chant, please say no, please say no, over and over, but he didn't. He had listened to his own words and couldn't disagree with them as much as he wanted to. John realized they really did make a good team.

"I'd love to," she replied softly. She reached out and took his hand. "Thank you, John. Thank you."

"You're welcome, Jessica," John replied. Jessica got a strange smile on her face.

"Call me Jess," she replied, pushing her hair back behind her right ear and smiling at him. "All my friends do." John was slightly confused. Sam walked up with Chet. No, that wasn't quite the right way to describe it. Sam leading Chet would be a better description.

"So?" Sam asked. John turned to Chet.

"We need to put the band back together," John said. Chet smiled.

"We're puttin' the band back together!" Chet exclaimed, nodding. John was just glad he didn't start flashing the rock and roll sign while he said it. Jessica rolled her eyes and sighed.

"That is the most overused saying in the history of the world," Jessica said to Sam. Sam nodded sagely.

"What else can you expect from these two?" Sam asked. The senator and Trip walked up to join them. "Have you two heard the good news? The three of them are going to continue as a team." Trip watched the senator.

"Excellent!" the senator proclaimed. Trip nodded.

"Great," he said, not quite as enthusiastically, not wanting to give his true feelings away. Before anyone could say anything, the New Year's countdown began. When zero was reached, John kissed Sam, the senator and Trip shook hands, and Jessica kissed Chet on his cheek. Everyone in the group was shaking hands or giving each other a kiss on the cheek. As Auld Lang Syne began, John and Jessica found themselves with their backs to each other. They turned to face each other, not realizing who it was behind them. Jessica started to lean in to kiss John, as John quickly stuck his hand out. Jessica stopped, and John had a look of horror on his face that he had embarrassed her. They both felt a hand on their shoulders and both turned to see Sam, smiling at them.

"It's okay, John," Sam said. "It's New Year's, and she's a friend." John looked trapped. That was when Jessica saved him.

"No," Jessica said, sticking out her hand. "Friends?" John smiled.

"Friends," he replied, taking her hand. Sam stood beside them, shaking her head.

"Well, at least hug the lady!" Sam said. Jessica shrugged, and she hugged John. Sam went to hug someone else. John went to break the hug when he found Jessica had him held tight.

"She made you take me, didn't she?" Jessica whispered into his ear.

"She did," John whispered back. "But she's right. You're great at what you do, and you do watch my back." John broke the hug; his hand was still on her back and hers on his. "This is me, offering you the spot. There is no pressure from Sam, just me, offering you a spot on the team." John thought he saw a tear in her eye.

"I'd like to be on your team, John," Jessica replied. John nodded. They hugged again and were quickly joined by others in the New Year's celebration. Sam watched from a little ways away from the group with the senator beside her.

"I think this is where they say something like, 'and now you know the rest of the story,'" Sam said to the senator. Jeremiah chuckled. "Thank you for finding someone to watch his back, Jeremiah. It means a lot to me." Jeremiah nodded and gave her a slight bow. They stood there a second, watching them when Jeremiah leaned in close.

"Forgive me for overstepping my bounds if I am, ma' dear, but who's going to watch her watching him?" the senator asked. Sam chuckled and turned toward him.

"Explain to me what it is about that man," she said to the senator. Jeremiah laughed out loud.

"You married the boy, not me!" he replied. Sam nodded and turned back toward the group.

"I trust her, Jeremiah. I don't know why, but I trust her with my life, the same way I do John," she said where only he could hear her.

"John would never hurt you, ma'dear," Jeremiah said softly. Sam turned and smiled at him.

"Neither would she, Jeremiah," Sam replied with a hint of a smile on her face, turning back to watch the three together that would become a tight knit team. "Neither would she."

Now
John's Apartment

Chapter 94

Jessica finished the chapter and looked up at John with a smile on her face and tears in her eyes. John was watching her with that irritating smirk on his face, while managing to look quite proud of himself.

"Not bad, Mr. Fowler," she admitted. "Not bad at all. With all we've been through over the last several years, I had kinda forgotten how much good we did that first time." John smiled at Jessica.

"So we can end this foolishness?" John asked. Jessica smiled and shook her head, enjoying watching the smug look fall off of John's face.

"I know an agent, and she's going to read the manuscript," Jessica said. "I'm thinking you need a pen name of some sort to publish under. I was thinking of someone that no one has ever heard of. How about the name, David Carner?" John groaned and rolled his eyes.

"Enough," he said, throwing his hands up in defeat. "Do what you want with it, but I've met all the conditions you and Trip laid out in front of me. I get to return to the FBI." It wasn't a question.

"Yes, John," Jessica said, nodding. "You have met all of the conditions, and now you can return to the FBI. But we have a decision to make. What do we do about the girl and the Moores?" John sucked in the inside of his left cheek, thinking. He slightly bobbed his head from side to side, thinking.

"We tell the Moores, and we go from there," John said, never looking up at Jessica. Jessica sat for a second, absentmindedly nodding. She then got up, walked over to

John, and took his hands in her hands. John continued to stare off to the side. Jessica moved her head around until she got in his line of sight. There were tears in his eyes.

"You didn't cheat on her John. You never acted for a minute on your feelings. Sam didn't begrudge how you felt," she said softly. John gave her an incredulous look.

"I know I didn't, Miss Hot-to-Trot," John replied. Jessica nearly burst out laughing from his reply. "I'm not upset about me and you. I'm worried about Amanda," John continued. "She knows nothing about her mother and only whatever lies her father has filled her head with." Jessica, still smiling, squeezed his hands.

"Apparently, Kenneth Nichols is not the man everyone seems to think he is," Jessica replied.

"We don't know that yet," John said.

"You mean we don't have evidence," she replied with a twinkle in her eyes. "You know," Jessica said, pushing his chest lightly with her forefinger. John couldn't help but grin.

"Yeah, I do," John replied. The grin left his face. "I just wish there was something I could have done for her. She was raised by him all this time, and now, she hates everything about me. I mean, she'll never be my daughter, but I feel like I owe Sam." Jessica looked at John lovingly. Here was a man who had no relation to his wife's daughter. Here was a man that didn't even know the girl, and yet, he was willing to do whatever he could for her.

"You didn't know," Jessica said softly. Suddenly, like a lightning bolt, it hit her what Sam had said to Jessica at the gravesite. She looked up at John.

"John, I know what Sam meant when I saw her at the gravesite when we got married," Jessica blurted out. John looked confused.

"When I saw her, she told me something," Jessica admitted. "She said to tell you 'it's not her, fault.' But, what was weird was I thought I had seen her earlier across the cemetery. Obviously, it was Amanda."

"It's not her fault," John repeated, nodding. He began to pace the room. "So, the way she is now, it's not her fault." He looked over at Jessica who nodded for him to continue. "So, it's the person's fault who raised her this way."

"Kenneth Nichols," Jessica said. John nodded.

"And if that's the case, then Kenneth's father falsified Amanda's death," John said. "Jessica, we've got to get those lab reports rushed and go see him." Jessica nodded and headed to the phone to call Trip and get the ball rolling on everything. John nodded absently and glanced over at the window. He felt it. He walked over to the window to look down at the street. There stood Amanda looking up at him from her normal spot. John waved, surprising Amanda, but instead of fleeing like she normally did when John thought he saw her, a smug look covered her face, and she waved with her fingers. John smiled and nodded. She then pointed at him with her forefinger and thumb like a gun and made a shooting motion. She blew on her forefinger like she was blowing away smoke. John had his famous smug smirk on his face and slowly shook his head no.

Jessica, noticing John, came over to stand beside him. As soon as Amanda saw Jessica, the look on Amanda's face turned to pure hatred. She turned and walked away. John and Jessica watched her go.

"John," Jessica said, almost pleading. "We have to go after her. We have to help her."

"Not yet," John replied, never taking his eyes off Amanda heading down the street. "Soon, Jessica, but not yet." As John watched her walk away, he couldn't help but feel Sam watching them. "We'll save her Sam. We'll save her," he said quietly as Jessica began to explain into the phone to Trip what was going on.

The End . . .For Now.

Author's note:

I started writing this book in December of 2012. I was very close to finishing when on April 15th, 2013, a tragedy occurred; bombs went off at the Boston Marathon. Now while an explosion at a SEC football game is not the same as what happened that day, it was enough to make me stop and pause. What I was writing was close enough to the tragedy that I wondered if I was doing the right thing by continuing the book. In my original story, people were going to die in the explosion. It would be these senseless deaths that united the team together. The team was going to work together to stop these kinds of events from happening. As I sat on the 15th of April and tried to ignore the news, I kept thinking about how it wasn't right. People were simply enjoying life, and now they were dead because of a senseless act of violence and terror.

The next morning, I honestly thought about tossing the entire book, but in my mind I kept thinking, "You can't let terror win." I posted on my private Facebook page how I felt and that I was thinking about starting over with the book. A friend, Clint Bragg, who has before made small suggestions that have heavily influenced the book, said something that stuck with me. Writing is my escape from reality, writing is my release, and today, in my world, the good guys won. I think I worked into the book how the threat of what almost happened helped shape the team. If not, I'm sorry, but today, the good guys won.